MW01118203

Zedalla™
Rescuing Oceans

Created by Darci Fredricks
Written and Illustrated by Joanna J. Robinson

Copyright © 2020 by Everyday Heroes.
All rights reserved. This book or any portion thereof
may not be reproduced or used in any manner whatso-
ever
without the express written permission of the publisher,
except for the use of brief quotations in a book review.

Printed in the United States of America

First Printing, October 2020

ISBN 978-1-7360501-0-1

Published by Everyday Heroes - Zedalla™ book series
Created by: Darci Fredricks

Author and Illustrator: Joanna J. Robinson

Cover Design: Lisa Vega
(Credit to Shutterstock for cover images of
turtle, whale, and various spot art);
cover character art by Joanna J. Robinson.

For my nephew Nolan, for whom we did not do a great job setting up with a healthy planet. I look forward to seeing how much better your generation does for each other and the animals that have to live with our choices.
-With hope, Auntie Darci

This book is also dedicated to all the Everyday Heroes who make our world a better place.
Thank you.

Dear Reader,

Thanks for choosing to read this important book!

Growing up as part of a lower-income family in the Midwest, I always dreamed of seeing the ocean and swimming with the amazing creatures that lived there. Thanks to my family's support, helpful resources available to me, and my own determination and hard work, I have been fortunate enough to travel the world and swim with singing whales, curious turtles, colorful fishes, and graceful sharks.

Through these amazing experiences, I have learned that I have a responsibility to give a voice to the beings I want to protect. So, I created Zedalla! She represents all the independent, smart, empathetic, passionate, and powerful children in the world. When she witnesses something negative about her neighborhood or another place in the world, she learns about it with her friends, and together, they take quick action towards positive change.

Zedalla and her friends are what I call Everyday Heroes. They are not politically powerful and they are not rich or famous. They take small, important actions each day to improve themselves and the world around them. They risk being inconvenienced in order to be better stewards for their community. They take positive action because it is the right thing to do, not because someone is watching. They are Everyday Heroes and you can be one, too!

Think about what YOU can do to make the world a better place for everybody then GO DO IT! Check out the back of this book for ideas on how to better serve your community today!

Thank you for taking the time to read about rescuing oceans!

Darci

Acknowledgments

A VERY special thank you to our awesome community reviewers and editors. Your detailed feedback early on in the creation of this story really helped Zedalla, Olivia, Nick, and Tess make it a unique and meaningful adventure!

Rachel Kaperick

Jacob Reyes

Reed Ross

James Jarc

Dasha Fruzyna

Bill Freeman

Ginny Kaperick

Jerry Jarc

ELIZABETH AND CATHY

Janet Schroeder

Maggie Gildea and Mary Van De Walle

KELLY F.

Sarah K.

Emily Padavick

JESSICA KEPSCHULL

Eileen Jarc

Amelie Creten

The Meyer Family

Table of Contents

Chapter 1
The Bracelet

Ding-Dong! Zedalla quickly swallowed her mouthful of hot chips and shouted, "I got it!" She ran to the front door where she found Grandma G smiling and waving enthusiastically.

"Can't stay but a minute," she said, hugging Zedalla with her right arm. She held a bag in her left hand that was overflowing with who-knows-what. "How's my girl? I missed you so much."

"I'm good. I missed you, too, Grandma. How was your trip?" asked Zedalla, hugging her tightly with one arm.

Grandma G was fresh off the plane from her trip to India.

"SO good, baby. I can't wait to tell you about it, but I am beat. I gotta get home and get some rest, but I just wanted to stop by and see your smiling face and bring you a special gift. I found it at an open-air market."

As she dug inside her bag, mom and dad Jones appeared and welcomed Grandma G home with kisses on the cheek. Then she pulled out a small, velvety red pouch with a pull tie at the top. She handed it to Zedalla, whose eyes lit up.

Inside, Zedalla found a bracelet with four beautiful gemstones. They were still rough around the edges, as if they had been handpicked straight from the earth. There were four colors – pink, red, blue, and orange.

"I love it! It is beautiful!" beamed Zedalla, "Thank you so much!" She hugged Grandma G with two arms this time. Then she tried it on her wrist. Perfect fit.

She was admiring the stones up close and just as Grandma G was telling her about them, each color flashed to show its color. Zedalla thought she was seeing things, so she asked if Grandma G had seen the gems flicker, too.

"Oh, that's probably the light bouncing off of them. These gems have unique cuts and angles in them so when sunlight hits them, they sparkle and shine a little," suggested Grandma G. "That's one reason I thought you'd like the bracelet."

That sounded simple enough, and made sense, but still, Zedalla was pretty sure the flicker was more than sunlight.

It seemed like it was coming from inside the gem. Oh well.

She accepted Grandma G's explanation for now. She'd look more closely if the gems flickered again.

It was so colorful and sparkly. She imagined that it was completely and 100% original. She was sure there wasn't another one like it in the entire world.

Grandma G explained that the old man who sold the bracelet said it was very special. Magical even. He gave Grandma G a small piece of paper with a message about the gems, which still smelled like curry and patchouli.

Synchronicity of Spirit

Passion

Empathy   Creativity

Wonderment

When the qualities are balanced and harmonious, magical things can happen.

Zedalla didn't know exactly what the message meant, or what kind of magic the bracelet might bring. That was fine. She liked the bracelet. In fact, she loved the bracelet, mainly because it was a gift from Grandma G.

She hoped the gems might do something, but she really didn't even know what to hope for, other than balance and harmony. Zedalla read and reread the message.

Synchronicity of Spirt. There were four stones with labels – Passion, Wonderment, Creativity, and Empathy. At the bottom of the paper it had another sentence that read, '*When the qualities are balanced and harmonious, magical things can happen.*'

She'd have to think about the meaning of this message a bit more. Maybe she would look up some of the words in the dictionary, just to be sure of what they meant. She had faith that it would make sense at some point.

She flipped the paper over. The backside explained more about the name of the gems, so she read that a few times, too.

Meaning of the Gemstones

Ruby – Passion, strength, and leadership

Rose Quartz – Empathy, compassion, and kindness

Carnelian – Creativity, imagination, and resourcefulness

Lapis Lazuli – Wonderment, curiosity, and intelligence

Then she put the paper back inside the pouch, pulled it closed, and kept it, just in case. And, the velvety pouch was so soft! It was just as cool as the bracelet.

This unique bracelet was perfect for Zedalla. Grandma G was always telling Zedalla that she was "one-of-a-kind," and Zedalla liked knowing that she was not like anybody else. She liked being different. It was also a huge compliment coming from someone she admired so much.

Zedalla aspired to be like Grandma G in so many ways. First, Zedalla hoped to become a great adventurer and world traveler, too. Second, she wanted to have Grandma G's amazing, positive energy. And third, Zedalla wanted to do important things that she believed would make the world better and follow her dreams, just like Grandma G.

She inspired Zedalla just by her example. She had so many interests and ideas that Zedalla could hardly keep up. She tried anyway.

Grandma G (the G was short for Gertie, which was short for Gertrude) was one of Zedalla's favorite people. Whenever Grandma G was around, she was smiling. Or laughing. Or both. Her eyes even twinkled a bit.

Luckily, Grandma G was around a lot. She lived close by – not a walkable distance, but still very close. She claimed it was just a "hop, skip, and jump" away.

It was obvious that Zedalla was one of Grandma G's favorite people, too. She stopped by all the time, she attended Zedalla's school events, and spent time sitting on the porch and chatting with Zedalla whenever she could.

"I can't get enough of you, Z. I just love seeing you grow," she'd tell Zedalla.

Sometimes, Zedalla would just listen to her talk about life. Grandma G was like a movie star, a comedian, and a magician all wrapped up into one person. She was captivating.

When she retired from her career as a teacher, and soon after Grandpa died, Grandma G vowed that she was going to "see the world."

She would say things like, "I don't want to die sitting in my recliner watchin' soaps. I've got places to go, people to see, and life to live." And that's exactly what she does.

Grandma G connected with some youthful, old ladies who were always going on wild adventures to foreign places. They had so much fun together.

After each trip, Grandma G would visit Zedalla's family. She'd tell a few stories about where she went and what she did, she'd show a bunch of pictures, and then she'd dig into her giant purse and pull out a gift for Zedalla.

It was always something special.

So far, Zedalla had collected a jewelry tray from Bali; a mini, marble hippopotamus from Africa; and a hand-stitched purse from Bangladesh.

And now, a beautiful gem bracelet from India.

Today's visit was shorter than most. Grandma G couldn't wait to give Z her bracelet, but she was also exhausted from a long plane ride. She gave a short report of her trip – just the highlights. Then Grandma G hugged Z again and promised to come back to tell more tales of her journey.

(Spoiler alert: she wanted to show Zedalla some silly selfies she took by India's most famous landmarks.)

As she was leaving, she reminded Zedalla about the power of the gems. "You'll see why it's special when the elements are in harmony. Trust me."

Chapter 2
Horrifying News

After Grandma G left, Zedalla started on her homework. *Why was there so much to do? Ugh.* She worked for a long time, breaking for mom's chicken and cheesy potatoes dinner, then it was back to work.

Meanwhile, her parents cleaned up the kitchen and sat down to watch the news. There was never anything good on the news, at least it didn't seem like it. Today was no different.

Zedalla sat at the kitchen table where she could see the TV in the living room. She was supposed to be concentrating on her work, but that wasn't always easy.

She was stuck on a word problem about ridiculous amounts of bananas and round-trip travel by boat to Monkey Island. She was busy sketching a monkey when she heard the news reporter say that a disturbing discovery has been made in the Pacific Ocean.

Ooooh, sounds juicy, thought Zedalla, who was always curious about things.

Her older twin brothers, who were never home, called her 'nosey,' but she called it 'inquisitive' and 'interested.' She stretched across the table to see and hear better as the news report continued.

A grim picture of a very large whale flashed across the screen. Zedalla's mother gasped and put her hand over her mouth. "Oh my gosh…" she whispered.

Zedalla couldn't help it – sitting still was so hard! She just had to find out what was going on. She hopped out of her chair and dashed to the living room.

"What is it? What happened?" she asked eagerly.

The headline at the top of the screen read: Plastic Peril. The reporter explained that a whale had washed up on shore and was dead. Scientists investigated to find out how it died, and they discovered over two hundred pounds of plastic and trash inside the whale's stomach!

As soon as she saw the whale, Zedalla gasped and her jaw dropped. She had never seen anything like it before. She could hardly believe her eyes.

Not only was it unbelievable, but it was horrifying and sad and confusing – all at the same time.

How could this happen? Zedalla wondered.

She had so many questions but she couldn't seem to get any words out, so she just stammered, "Wha…I mean…wh…how… did… I just…ugh."

"Pitiful," said Dad, shaking his head in disgust.

"Shhh," said Mom. "Let's listen and find out how this happened."

Turns out, the whale had mistaken the colorful, plastic garbage in the ocean for food. Unfortunately, the whale had consumed so much plastic and no real food, that it died of malnutrition. That poor whale didn't stand a chance against all that junk in the ocean.

Zedalla knew that plastic was in a lot of things she used, but she didn't know that plastic could be so deadly. She knew it was durable, long-lasting, and strong. But now she was seeing a new side of plastic – the bad side of plastic. And worse: the deadly side.

This whale story made Zedalla want to know more about so many things. She loved animals and creatures of all kinds – from fleas (okay, maybe not fleas) and ants to whales and everything in between. She wanted to know how she could help so this kind of thing wouldn't happen again.

The reporter continued, "Numerous ocean animals are dying as a result of human plastic pollution. Animals get caught in plastic fishing nets, or digest plastic. Plastic has dramatically interfered with the ocean habitat and the animals who live there."

Zedalla wondered if this plastic problem had anything to do with global warming. She knew climate change was a real threat to animals and the environment. And now she was learning that plastics can affect animal habitats, too. She wondered what the connection was between plastics and global warming. They must be related, but how?

All of a sudden, the red gem on her bracelet pulsed. She felt it vibrate, too. She looked and, just like before, it glowed. *I'm not seeing things! I was right – it IS glowing! What does it mean?* she wondered.

Zedalla refocused back to the news story. She felt sad for the ocean animals. No more whales should have to suffer. No more dolphins or seals should have to die from eating plastic. No more turtles should be trapped in plastic fish netting or plastic packaging. No more animals should lose their habitats because of plastic.

Mostly, Zedalla felt worried that the plastic problem would only get worse if she didn't do something. She couldn't just sit there and watch these unavoidable tragedies happen.

Zedalla finished her homework quickly, packed up her bookbag, and ran up to her room. She had to find some answers.

21

Just as she was getting started with her research, Tess FaceTimed her. After all, it was about that time. Tess called nearly every night at around 7:30, just to check in. That's what best friends often do.

"Hey! What's up?" asked Tess.

She showed up on the screen normally, but with a robotic voice. She was always finding new gifs, memes, and apps to spice up the conversation. Tess was smart and techy like that.

Zedalla was too distracted to appreciate the robotic cover, so she jumped right into what she was thinking as she paced around the room.

"Check this out," began Zedalla. "I just saw this story on the news about a whale that died and scientists found plastic trash in its belly. Isn't that just, I don't know, completely sickening?"

"What in the world? That's sick. Poor thing," said Tess.

"I know that the polymers in plastic are not exactly nutritious, but I'm guessing the whale mistook plastic for krill. To be honest, I didn't know plastic could be so dangerous. And for sure I didn't realize that animals would eat it."

Zedalla admitted, "Me neither. I'm about to research online. I will let you know what I find."

"Okay, cool. Now you've got me curious. I'm going to look up some stuff, too. We should share our findings tomorrow," suggested Tess.

Zedalla could always count on Tess to get excited about important issues like this. She was very supportive. And, Tess was super smart when it came to science and research. Zedalla knew she would double her knowledge about plastic and whales overnight.

"Great idea!" answered Zedalla. "By the way, nice robot voice. Talk to you tomorrow."

"Thank you for your compliment, friend. Must research plastic now. Later," said Tess. She buzzed, beeped, then hung up.

Zedalla plopped down on her bed and flipped open her laptop. She googled things like, 'Plastic in the ocean' and 'What is plastic?' and 'Whales eating plastic.'

She scanned page after page. She clicked on links and more links. She was lost down a rabbit hole of information and she couldn't believe what she was discovering.

Chapter 3
All About Plastic

Zedalla was amazed by what she was reading. And, disgusted. Of course, you can't believe everything you read on the internet. She browsed and swiped between different sites and gathered all kinds of information about plastic. And, she made sure that she checked and double-checked her facts with different sites. She did not want to be learning the wrong information.

So many things are made with plastic, but what was plastic anyway?

"That's what I need to find out before I learn anything else," she exclaimed.

She googled, 'What is plastic?' and 'How is plastic made?' She discovered that plastics are a mix of many chemicals made by humans.

Zedalla's mind wandered. She imagined mad scientists

and crazy chemists working together in a lab with beakers and test tubes, mixing different-colored chemical potions to make plastic...

She doodled...

She imagined the occasional explosion and puffs of pink smoke, and fizzy, oozing spills of random gooey liquids...

Then, like a cartoon character recovering from being hit in the head with a hammer, she shook her head back and forth and refocused.

No wonder plastic lasts forever, she thought. *And, no wonder it can do so much damage to the environment and animals. And people for that matter!*

Zedalla thought about all the things made of plastic: straws, spoons and forks, cups, bowls, water bottles, soda bottles, grocery bags, food containers, wrappers and packaging for so many different kinds of products...

She looked around her room. There was – literally – plastic everywhere! Laptop, phone charger, desk, chair, water bottle, lamp, sunglasses, lip gloss...

Next, Zedalla read about single-use plastic, or plastic that is only used one time. *Duh. Single-use. One time. That makes sense.*

But the crazy thing was that more than 40% of all plastic is used only once before it is thrown away – that's almost half of all the plastics people use!

Then Zedalla remembered something. When she went to her brother's game, she bought a soda. It came in a plastic cup with a plastic straw. She drank the drink then threw away the cup and the straw.

She used the plastic for less than 10 minutes. And now, it was probably in the environment where it will stay for decades. Zedalla shuddered at the thought that her plastic could have ended up inside that whale. Gulp.

She scrolled for more information and read aloud, "Some plastic ends up in landfills, which are like disgusting mountains of trash, and some plastic ends up in the environment. The plastic might break down into smaller and smaller pieces called micro-plastics, which can be ingested by both animals and people.

"Yikes! I hope I've never ingested plastic," Zedalla groaned, rubbing her belly.

It was getting late and Zedalla's eyes were starting to droop. She had been staring at the computer for way too long.

She let out a big, loud yawn.

Just then, her mom appeared in the doorway and said, "Why don't you bookmark that page so you can check it out tomorrow? You should start getting ready for bed."

"Okay," moaned Zedalla as she rolled off her bed to find her pajamas.

She had to admit – she was tired. Sometimes the whole bedtime routine was energy-zapping. Couldn't she just hire someone to brush her teeth and wash her face for her? Maybe Tess could invent a robot to do that...

Before turning off her light, Zedalla carefully removed her special bracelet from Grandma G. She admired it again and set it on her jewelry tray. She planned to take good care of it. She didn't want it to get broken or lost in her swamp of sheets, pillows, stuffed animals, and blankets. If that happened, she might never find it again.

Then she turned off the light, slumped into bed, and before her head even hit the pillow, she was out.

Chapter 4
Do You Believe in Magic?

The next morning, Zedalla woke up and got ready for school as usual. She took a quick shower and threw on whatever clothes were clean and not-so wrinkled.

It was springtime in the Midwest. That meant one thing: you never know what you were going to get when it came to the weather. The only thing you could count on was unpredictability.

Instead of worrying about fashion, Zedalla chose layers of colors and patterns that she liked. Nobody cared if she matched, and neither did she. Luckily, she was one of those people who looked cool without really trying.

Exhibit A: one star-spangled sock and one donut sock. That was just Zedalla.

She had more important things to think about.

As she was pouring herself a bowl of cereal, she noticed her bare wrist and realized that she had already forgotten to put on her new bracelet.

"Holy guacamole! I've had it one day and I already forgot!" she hollered.

She ran back upstairs, grabbed it off her jewelry tray, and put it on. Phew! She watched it sparkle in the morning sunlight. The rays bounced off the colorful gems and created the coolest pattern on her bedroom wall. That kind of sparkle was definitely different from what she saw yesterday.

Since Zedalla's dad and twin brothers had already left for the day, Zedalla and her mom exchanged pleasantries while she finished eating breakfast.

At exactly 8:17, Mrs. Jones shuffled Zedalla out the door with a kiss on her forehead, saying, "Have a good day, love you, Z."

"Love you, too, Mom," said Zedalla, hugging her mom tightly around her waist. Then she skipped down the sidewalk to meet Tess.

Not only were they best friends, but Tess and Zedalla lived just two streets away from one another. And they went to the same school. Tess always waited for Zedalla at the corner where their streets intersected, and they'd walk together. Or skip. Or run.

Or however they felt like getting to school that day.

"Hey, Z. So, what did you find out in your research last night?" asked Tess.

"SO MUCH," answered Zedalla. "But there's so much more I want to know. Apparently, there are certain parts of the oceans where trash gets stuck, like TONS of trash. The trash stays in those spots called gyres (pronounced jie-ers), and it swirls around in circles and never disappears."

"That's crazy," said a wide-eyed Tess. "I wonder why it just goes in circles like that. I assume it has something to do with the ocean tides and the cycles of the moon." Tess paused and touched her temple. "Note to self: investigate gyres."

Just then Zedalla felt her wrist vibrating. She looked down and saw that the blue gem on her bracelet was pulsing faintly, but it only glowed on and off for a moment. Zedalla looked up to see if Tess noticed but Tess wasn't even looking in her direction. She was deep in thought, staring at the trees and mumbling to herself about what to research next. Hmmm, last night it was the red stone that was lighting up. I wonder what made the blue stone do that.

Tess was smart. She was always asking questions and trying to figure things out. She wondered about everything. She was always hypothesizing and theorizing about how things work or why things happen before knowing the details. Her thinking was logical and strategic, so her theories often turned out to be correct.

Tess was a bit of a nerd, and she was more than okay with that. After all, chess club and math club were not groups that just anyone could join. Tess embraced her intelligence. She didn't flaunt it, and she was careful not to make anyone feel stupid. She never said, "I told you so." But she was nerdy and proud of it.

Despite her wisdom, Tess wasn't super confident in social situations, so she often followed Zedalla's charismatic lead. Zedalla was the social butterfly – she was friends with everyone. Zedalla had awesome ideas, but she often deferred to Tess when it came to technical and factual stuff.

That arrangement was fine with both of them. That's what made their friendship work so well.

"I clearly need to do more research, but it was getting late and I had to quit. What did you find out?" asked Zedalla.

"Some fishing companies that use plastic nets are irresponsibly abandoning them in the oceans. Those nets can be really dangerous for smaller sea animals, especially sea turtles. The plastic can get stuck around their necks and strangle them," explained Tess.

Zedalla stopped in her tracks. "What?! NO! You have got to be kidding me," she said in disbelief. "That's so sad!"

31

"It is sad. And sadly, I'm not kidding," said Tess, frowning. "But the good news is that some companies are inventing nets that will eventually dissolve in the ocean water. Dare I say, genius!"

"Were you two talking about me again? I heard someone say the word genius," interjected Nick, as he joined Tess and Zedalla on their way to school.

Nick lived close by and walked to school with the girls. He was like a brother to them – kind, protective, thoughtful, and definitely silly. He was always cracking them up. He was creative and clever, but not a genius. And, he embraced that.

"Oh, we were just talking about how plastics are dangerous for sea animals. I saw this report on the news last night about a whale that got plastic stuck in its stomach…" began Zedalla.

"I saw that, too!" shouted Nick. "That was no joke! I didn't realize plastic was such a big problem. It certainly was a problem for that whale."

"Yeah. I feel like we should do something, but I don't know exactly what. I am going to stop using so many plastic straws, and cups, and bags wherever and whenever I can," explained Zedalla.

"That's logical. I'll do that, too," said Tess.

"Yeah. I'm on it," agreed Nick. "Plus, I'll tell everyone I know to do the same thing."

"Perfect. Well, look at that! We're already making a difference," said Zedalla proudly.

Once they reached the school playground, they met up with Olivia. She had walked from her house on the opposite side of the school.

The four friends always climbed to the top of the tower and hung out until the bell rang.

It was their daily meeting spot. Over the years, they had discovered that it was quiet, surprisingly comfortable, and just far enough away from the little kids on the playground. It was the perfect place to catch up on the latest news.

"Hi, guys. What's up?" asked Olivia, who immediately sensed something atypical. "Wait, what's wrong?"

She noticed that the friends seemed different. They seemed... serious. And thoughtful. She wasn't sure exactly what was different, but she certainly needed to find out. She could read people well, and she knew something was off.

33

"Do you want to make a plastic pact with us?" asked Nick. "Did you see that thing about the whale? Did you know turtles are suffering?"

"Hold on. What do you mean?" asked Olivia, who had clearly missed out on part of the discussion and needed to know more.

Zedalla explained the whole plastic-problem-thing to Olivia (from the beginning). Of course, Olivia was cool with the plastic pact, now that she understood what they were talking about. Zedalla knew how much Olivia liked animals, so it was a no-brainer that she would participate.

In fact, when Zedalla broke the news about the whale with plastic in its belly, she thought she saw a tiny tear running down Olivia's cheek. Olivia was thoughtful and sensitive like that.

"Seriously?!" said Olivia in horrified disbelief, "That is the WORST thing I could possibly imagine. That news makes me feel so sad. Sea animals are sooooo cute and they don't deserve that. They need a safe and clean habitat. That's it! I refuse to use plastic ever again." She crossed her arms in front of her.

"Well, let's just start with little steps," said Zedalla, "I mean, think about it – many things we need every day have parts made of plastic. It has some good qualities. But, we can start by cutting down on plastic use, especially plastics we only use one time – like straws, cups, and bags."

Nick agreed. "Yep. I'm totally in. Let's be honest, I'm already part of so many other problems, I don't need to be part of the plastic problem, too."

The girls knew Nick was joking and they giggled. He was always being silly and teasing himself. Somehow, that made him extra loveable.

Zedalla continued, "If nothing else, at least we won't be adding to the plastic problem. We have to figure out how to stop plastics from getting into lakes and oceans. We've got to help those animals. And we need to clean up the oceans for humans, too. But, I'm not exactly sure how just yet."

Olivia, Tess, and Nick knew this was the beginning of a plastic revolution. They watched Zedalla with fascination, imagining the cogs and gears inside her brain busy at work. They admired this quality in their friend. They had seen it many times before, and it was always fun to watch.

Zedalla was always thinking BIG. Making little changes was all fine and good because little changes DO matter, but Zedalla wanted BIG change.

"We should get together again after school. We can brainstorm," said Tess. "I bet we can come up with some great ideas." Everyone agreed to that plan.

The bell rang. The friends exited the tower.

Together, they made their way toward the door with all the other students.

Zedalla walked a little slower than the others. She was busy thinking about next steps in this plastic adventure. As she thought about big changes she could make, she felt her bracelet vibrate – just like it had done the day before. She looked at it. The red gem was glowing!

Now she had something else to think about. Why was just the red gem glowing? Why did the blue gem glow earlier? What caused it glow right now?

So far, Zedalla couldn't figure it out. Right now, it didn't matter though. She had to focus on her schoolwork first, and then the plastic problem, and then she could try to solve the mystery of the glowing gems. Until then, she admired the beautiful, red glow.

Chapter 5
Zapped to Another World

Time seemed to drag on during the day. Zedalla's mind wandered. A LOT. It was hard to focus on math, or science, or spelling, or anything, when there was a plastic crisis happening in the world.

In science, she was supposed to be researching about the squirrel monkey's habitat for her report. Instead, Zedalla took an internet detour and discovered something called the Great Pacific Garbage Patch – a super-huge resting spot for 8 million tons of trash from all over the world.

Gross, she thought.

During math, she was supposed to be practicing her times tables with Mike S. Instead, she practiced telling him about single-use plastics and the Great Pacific Garbage Patch.

He just rolled his eyes.

In spelling, Zedalla was supposed to write and rewrite her spelling words five times each. She did. Then she added a few of her own words. And doodles. And drawings.

Spelling Words   Zedalla Jones

completion   correction   invention
completion   correction   invention
completion   correction   invention
completion   correction   invention
completion   correction   invention

prevention   inspection   pollution
prevention   inspection   pollution
prevention   inspection   pollution
prevention   inspection   pollution
prevention   inspection   pollution

distraction   Trash
distraction   Ocean
distraction   Gyre
distraction   Whale
distraction   Plastic

R.I.P. mr. whale

This is me being mad about all the plastic in the ocean.

Even lunch was a distraction. Zedalla couldn't help but notice all the plastic in the lunchroom. Trays. Straws. Wrappers. Baggies. More wrappers. Garbage bags. She nibbled on her apple, but she didn't have much of an appetite.

Finally, after language arts, gym, and health, the 3:00 bell rang. The friends met up again at the top of the tower on the playground. They dropped their bookbags and sighed at the same time.

"What a day," said Nick, collapsing to the ground.

Without giving her friends a chance to breathe, Zedalla grabbed her notebook and her favorite purple gel pen. She flipped to the last page and turned her notebook upside-down.

As she explained what she had been thinking about all day, puffy gray clouds rolled in and the sky grew dark. Everything had a weird, eerie, yellowish glow. The friends glanced at the sky.

They watched and waited. The clouds moved slowly, and the sun peeked through again. The sun beam landed right on the playground tower like a gigantic spotlight.

The light was so bright! It shined right on Zedalla's colorful bracelet. The sun's rays bounced off the gemstones.

They looked at each other out of the corners of their eyes. This was weird. Each gem color reflected onto one of her friend's faces. Nick looked orange, Olivia looked pink, and Tess looked blue. Zedalla looked red.

The sky grew dark again. The clouds moved faster. The wind picked up.

When the clouds separated, the sunlight bounced off Zedalla's bracelet again. Same thing. Four faces. Four colors – the same colors as before.

It was as if each color was meant specifically for one of the friends. The sun went behind the dark clouds again, but the wind picked up even faster.

"Whoa," said Tess. "What's going on? Usually, I can come up with some sort of scientific explanation for why something is happening, but this has got me completely stumped."

"That's my new bracelet," said Zedalla. "When my grandma gave it to me yesterday, she said it could be magical. I never expected the magic to happen right away!"

"Well, something's happening now," said Nick.

Olivia noticed that the sun was about to peek out from the clouds again. "Let's see what happens next time the sun shines on it," she said.

Nick and Tess agreed. Zedalla held her bracelet out in front of her. They all watched and waited.

The clouds parted and the sun beamed down on them.

This time, it was blinding. Each friend held up a hand to stop the light from shining in their eyes.

"NOW, what's happening?" asked Nick, "It's blinding me – aaaaah!"

"I don't know!" screamed Zedalla, "Maybe this is part of the magic my grandma was talking about!"

"Well, what kind of magic is this? And what is it going to do?" asked Olivia, who was a little more than slightly nervous. She wasn't fond of surprises, or the unknown.

"I'm not sure I like this kind of magic," she added, "I prefer the other kind of magic, like genie magic, or whatever it's called. I mean, where are the beautiful unicorns, cute little fuzzy bunnies, and fairies, and rainbows?"

"I have no idea!" exclaimed Zedalla.

Tess yelled so the friends could hear her over the wind, "Hold on! The barometric pressure is rising. The wind is getting even stronger!"

They grabbed hands and held on to each other.

Suddenly, there was a flash of bright light. Glittery dust swirled around them. They closed their eyes. There was a strange whizzing-whirring noise that ended with a *zoop*.

41

Almost as quickly as it began, everything became calm again. The dark clouds disappeared. The sun came back out. Even Olivia's hair settled back to where it belonged. Well, almost.

When everything stopped moving, the friends rubbed their eyes and looked around. They definitely were NOT at the top of the playground tower anymore – that was for sure – but they didn't know exactly where they were. Wherever they were, it was hot. And humid. The sun was out, and it was scorching. The air smelled like a clean sea breeze. They could hear waves gently crashing on a nearby shore.

Chapter 6
Mystery Location

"Where in the world are we?" asked Tess.

"No idea," answered Zedalla, looking around. "Clearly, we're at a beach... somewhere."

"I don't know where we are either," said Olivia. "And that's just great. We are probably smack dab in the middle of nowhere."

"Well, we're not nowhere. We are somewhere," said Zedalla matter-of-factly.

"I know where we are!" shouted Nick with such confidence that the girls stopped and looked to him for an answer. "Lost!" he said, "We're lost – that's exactly where we are. Lost."

"Thanks. That's very helpful. Not. There's only one way to find out where we are," said Zedalla. "We are just going to have to explore."

"Correction. There is another way to find out where we are. I can just check the GPS on my phone," suggested Nick.

Nick whipped out his phone, "Let's see. GPS... Open the app... location search... Wow! Apparently, I can get Wi-Fi here. Good thing. It shows that we are on Kahili Beach. It is the northernmost point of one of the small Hawaiian islands."

"Seriously?! I've always wanted to go to Hawaii! I'm so excited!" screamed Tess. "The flora and fauna are amazing here..."

Zedalla was quick to chime in, "Well, I don't know anything about flora and fauna, or exactly why we're here. Or, how we got here for that matter. There must be a reason..."

"I usually don't fall for magic, but if we can't explain how we got here with any facts or scientific causation, then maybe your bracelet really is magic after all," said Tess. "Your grandma is probably right. I mean, how else could we just end up half-way across the world in a matter of seconds? It's not physically or scientifically possible."

Zedalla smiled, "You're right. I can't explain it with any facts. It must have something to do with the gems on my bracelet – the way the sunlight was shining on them and reflecting a color back on us when we were in the tower."

"What do the gems have to do with anything? Why was I orange? What do the colors mean?" said Nick. "I'm so confused!"

44

"I don't know," said Zedalla. "I have a little paper about the gems at home, something about harmony and balance, but I don't remember what each color means."

Olivia added, "Okay, so, we don't know how we got here, why we are here, or what the gems mean.Please tell me that, somehow, this bracelet will magically transport us home when it's time. I can't handle being away from my animals for very long – they need me. Oh, man, I already miss their furry, little faces."

Olivia's family had two dogs, a ferret, several fish, and four cats. Olivia loved all animals and all of her family's animals, but the cats were her favorites.

"We will have to worry about getting home later. As the old saying goes, 'we'll cross that bridge when we come to it,'" said Tess. "For now, we have some exploring to do. And we've got to figure out why we're here."

"Right," agreed Zedalla, refocusing. "I wonder what Kahili Beach has to do with plastic…and…"

It was only a matter of seconds before Zedalla's mind caught up with her lips.

"Hold up! I just had the craziest thought. You know how I was telling you guys that the plastic ends up in those gyers, which are like spinning pools of water where the plastics get stuck? I wonder if there's a gyre around here!"

"Did you say there are gyros around here?" asked Olivia, who was always focused on food.

Zedalla continued "No, not gyro - gyre. I think it was off the coast of California, between Hawaii and Japan. I bet that's why we're here. We can see what this Great Pacific Garbage Patch looks like!"

Olivia added, "Maybe we can talk to the people who are already cleaning up the oceans. Maybe some of those teams you talked about are here doing actual clean-up work."

"Good point," said Nick. "And maybe we can even help with a clean-up. You never know, we might actually be able to help some animals, too."

"Awww," said the girls "Animals!"

"I hope we see some animals, but I hope we don't have to save any animals," said Olivia, "because that would mean that animals are in trouble."

"Agreed," said Zedalla. "First, we have to figure out where to go from here. I mean, look around. There's nothing but sand and trees and water. Hmm, which direction should we go?"

Tess looked around and made some quick calculations. She observed the placement of the sun in relation to the beach. Next, she assessed the wave patterns and estimated the angle of the tree shadows. Then she picked up a pinch of sand and let it fall, hoping to identify the direction of the wind. The friends watched her in amazement, not sure what she was doing or how her methods would help in deciding which way to go.

Meanwhile, Nick looked up Kahili Beach on his phone. It says this beach is good for swimming and snorkeling, fishing, surfing, and body boarding. Thank you, Google, for making me feel smart."

"It is pretty hot out here. I really could use a dip in the ocean," said Olivia.

"Not so fast," continued Nick, as he read on. "It says here that if the water is murky, you shouldn't swim because of jagged rocks and dangerous rip tides. Not to mention there might be random sea creatures that could sting us if we frighten them."

"That's true," said Olivia. "After all, the ocean is their home first. I'd hate to scare them, or hurt them, or put any animal in danger. We should respect all animals and where they live – whether it's on land or in the water."

As Olivia was speaking, Zedalla felt a familiar vibration. She looked down at her wrist. This time, the pink gemstone was glowing and pulsing!

Zedalla was starting to recognize some sort of connection between certain conversations with her friends and the pulsing of

47

gems on her magical bracelet. She hesitated to mention the flashing because she was still trying to piece together the timing and meaning behind it.

Right now, it was more important to focus on why they were here. Zedalla found some information about garbage patches on her phone. She read the main details aloud for her friends. "Garbage patches are found in the calm, stable centers of many of the world's ocean gyres. Even smaller bodies of water, such as the Mediterranean and North Seas, are developing their own garbage patches along heavily-trafficked shipping lanes."

"The Great Pacific Garbage Patch is an area that covers an estimated five million square miles of ocean – that's the same size as the U.S., Mexico, and Central America combined!"

"Woah!" said Nick. "That is ginormous!"

"Guys, check this out," said Zedalla. "This website says that eight million tons of plastic trash ends up in our oceans every year."

"Eight million tons? That sounds like a whole, whole, WHOLE lot of trash and plastic," said Olivia. "I can't even visualize how much that is. How do people use that much plastic? It's kind of ridiculous if you think about it."

"It IS ridiculous, even if you don't think about," joked Nick.

48

"Well, think about it this way," said Tess, "There are roughly 7.8 billion people in the world, right? And everyone uses plastic in some form, often just one time. Then most people throw it away. So it makes perfect sense that there would be that much plastic in the ocean. It IS totally ridiculous."

"That's why it's so important that each person cuts down on plastic use. It would probably really make a difference in the size of those gyres," said Zedalla.

"We will shrink the gyres!" shouted Nick, who was perched atop a nearby rock with his hand in the air, finger pointing to the sky, as if he were a superhero on some sort of quest for gyre justice. "But first, I must dump my shoes, for there is way too much sand in them."

The girls giggled. They needed a laugh after all this serious talk about trash.

Turns out, they were all ankle-deep in sand. The sand was really soft and powdery, and toasty warm. They shook out their shoes and socks, because, to be honest, sand between the toes when they're inside your shoes is not the best way to start an adventure.

The friends looked around. There were tons of plants, trees, and grasses. The landscape was beautiful.

Behind the beach was a lagoon. The lagoon was a smaller pool of water surrounded by land. Other than a few fish swimming around, it was calm and quiet.

Straight ahead, they observed nothing but ocean. Clear blue, calm, and it extended further than the eye could see.

"I feel like Gilligan trapped on an island," said Nick. "I hope we're not stuck here forever."

"Who's Gilligan?" asked Tess, who knew a lot about a lot of things, but had never heard of Gilligan.

"What?!?! You don't know... Gilligan? You know, *Gilligan's Island*? Oh man. Forget it," said Nick. He shook his head in disbelief.

"Yeah, but I hope it's not dangerous here," said Zedalla. "Sometimes islands have wild animals, like monkeys or snakes."

"Aww, monkeys!" said Olivia, "I would love to see a real monkey up close. I mean, if it was a friendly one, of course. Snakes? Not so much. I mean, cool animal and everything, but I would rather admire them from a distance."

"Totally agree," said Zedalla.

"I hope there's some sort of food source," added Olivia. "I never got my after-school snack."

Olivia rubbed her belly, which let out a tiny growl.

Just then, Zedalla noticed something washed up on the beach a few yards away. It sparkled in the sun.

Chapter 7
The Map to... X?

"Hey, I wonder what that is," Zedalla said, pointing to something in the sand.

She ran to the sparkly object and picked it up. It was a clear glass bottle. Inside was a rolled-up piece of paper. It had been yellowed by the sun.

"Ooh, ooh, I bet it's a secret message!" said Nick, "Get it out, get it out! Or, wait, maybe it's a map to a gold treasure..."

Zedalla shook the bottle and shook the bottle some more, but the paper didn't come out.

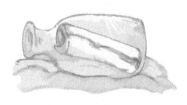

"How are we going to get this thing out?" she grumbled as she shook it like crazy.

"I bet we could use a small stick to pry it out," said Tess.

"Or, maybe we could fill it with water and the paper would float to the top," suggested Olivia, who quickly realized that wet paper would be hard to read, or that the water might smear the writing. "Oh, uh… Scratch that."

"Or, we could just break the bottle," suggested Nick, holding his head up with pride. "Captain Obvious to the rescue once again!" He patted himself on the back.

This time, his idea happened to be the best idea. Zedalla smacked her palm on her forehead. Duh.

Just then, the orange gem on her bracelet glowed and pulsed. Zedalla felt it, then she saw it. She wasn't surprised. But she was still a little confused. She made a mental note of when and where it happened then vowed to figure it out later.

She focused back on finding out what was inside the bottle. Everyone stepped back and Zedalla carefully broke the bottle on a nearby rock and removed the paper. Slowly and carefully she unrolled it…

Nick, Tess, and Olivia peered over Zedalla's shoulder, trying to get a good look at the paper.

"It IS a map!" Zedalla declared.

"What do you think the map is for – buried treasure?" wondered Nick, rubbing his hands together...

He imagined gold and money and jewels and…

"Well, there's the X and that usually means treasure," began Olivia. "But I kind of doubt it. I mean, I guess somebody could have buried a treasure long ago and it might still be there. There's only one way to find out."

Then, at the same time, they all said the exact same thing, "Follow the path toward the X."

Zedalla turned the map so that the beach was in front of them. She was usually good with directions, and she also knew her friends would step in and correct her if they thought she was way off.

"It looks like we need to go around a rock quarry first, and then through the tropical forest over there," Zedalla located the quarry then followed the path on the map with her finger.

"Well, let's get moving," said Olivia.

Suddenly Nick grabbed his heart and said, "Oh no… I'm… dying…" He wobbled left and right, then fell into the sand with his eyes closed. The girls stared at him for a good ten seconds.

He peeked through one eye and saw that they were all looking at him.

"Okay, okay, just kidding," he continued as he stood up. "I mean, my phone battery is dying. Hopefully we won't need technology much longer because I don't see any plugs or chargers around here."

The friends hadn't thought of that. They had to get on with their adventure. At least, back to some sort of civilization with electricity.

"Yikes! Onward!" exclaimed Zedalla. The friends headed toward the quarry.

Once they got closer, they admired the reddish-brown jagged edges that stuck out into the ocean. Carefully, they made their way around the rocks. On the other side, there was another beautiful beach.

They looked at the map again and noticed a path near a small cluster of rocks. They walked that way and, sure enough, they found the path.

"So far, so good," said Tess. "This map is pretty accurate, even though the scaling is slightly off."

They started down the path, which was soon overgrown with vines and prickly bushes.

"Ouch!" shouted Nick. "I'm being eaten alive by killer plants. Aaaaaah!"

The girls giggled again. Zedalla picked up a stick from nearby. It was not only the perfect walking stick, it was also the best vine-breaker and could be a protective weapon if they ran into any surprised monkeys or hungry snakes.

Nick and the others found sticks, too.

"Now we're ready," said Nick, swinging his stick like a ninja. "Eeeee-Yaaaaaah!"

They ventured further down the path, using their sticks to break through the vines and move the prickly bushes out of the way. If there were any snakes hanging out in the forest, their slithery bodies disappeared before the sticks could scare them. And, lucky for the friends, there were no monkeys waiting to mount a surprise attack.

They pressed on. After about 500 feet of overgrown vines, they came to a clearing. The path sloped up, and the friends trudged on, moaning and groaning most of the way.

It was hot. They had been walking and climbing and fending off branches. They were tired. By now they were all sweating, Olivia was still hungry, and they were all a little thirsty. Actually, A LOT thirsty.

"Are we there yet? I can't go much farther. I am soooo hungry," moaned Olivia, wiping sweat from her forehead.

"C'mon O, you can do this," said Zedalla. She reached in her backpack and handed Olivia a granola bar. "Here. Eat this."

"You mean to tell me you have had this in your backpack this whole time?" asked Olivia in disbelief. "I've been starving since we left school!"

"Sorry. Actually, not sorry. I was trying to conserve our resources," explained Zedalla. "Better now?"

Olivia gobbled up the granola bar as if she hadn't eaten in several days.She wiped granola crumbs from her shirt and rubbed her happy tummy. Then she responsibly stuffed the wrapper into her backpack, as not to add more trash into the environment.

"Much better," said Olivia, licking the melting chocolate from her lips. "Onward, my friends!"

Chapter 8
Timo and Mojo

At a clearing, they checked the map again.

"It looks like if we go that way," said Zedalla, pointing to the right, "we will run into a building. Maybe we can ask for help."

"Or, maybe the shop has water," said Nick, who stuck his tongue out and pretended like he was about to fall over. "I'm parched!"

"Yeah, yeah, I'll get you some water," said Zedalla, putting her arm around Nick's shoulder.

They all needed water. If they had any clue they'd be on this type of adventure, they might have prepared with the right provisions.

The building was not quite what they expected. It might not even be considered a building.

It was actually a tiki hut with a small
front counter.
The hand-painted sign out front
advertised snacks.

An older man stood near the counter in a small area of shade. He
was very thin and wore a wooden necklace with a tiki design on it.
His hair was scraggly, though hidden under
his hat, and he hadn't shaved in a while.
He wore a flowered shirt, shorts, and sandals.
He looked sandy, and a little dirty, and he
was super suntanned. It was clear he
was local to the area.

As the friends approached, he smiled,
showing a missing front tooth. His eyes lit up and
he welcomed the friends.

"E Komo Mai (Welcome! Enter)," he said repeatedly, and
very excitedly, gesturing with his arms for the children to come
closer.

"Apparently, he doesn't get out much," said Nick.

The girls giggled. Zedalla elbowed Nick in the ribs.

"Shhh," she gently scolded. "He seems really friendly,"
whispered Zedalla.

The man handed each of them a small, cone-shaped paper cup of water.

"But… we don't have any money," began Tess.

Before she could even finish explaining, the man smiled and said, "You don't need money. You can have it, for free – for free. Please. I can tell you need water. You must drink to hydrate."

"Are you sure? Thank you so much!" said Olivia.

"Yes, thank you!" said the others.

"Aloha," said the man. "A'ole pilikia, (pronounced Ah-ola poli kia), no problem."

"Aloha," the children repeated. "Thank you!"

"Hey, check it out," said Zedalla. "Paper cups! No plastic. This guy is on board with the plastic pact and he might not even know it."

Zedalla gave him a thumbs up.

Then the kind man offered the children dried banana chips in a small, brown paper bag and fresh pineapple chunks on wooden toothpicks. The friends were thankful for the tasty treats.

"These are good," said Olivia. She was still very hungry.

Zedalla had never had banana chips before but she was pleasantly surprised as well.

"These are good," Zedalla said. "And I bet they are good for you."

"Yep," said Tess. "They contain potassium, as well as other vitamins and nutrients."

"Agreed," said Nick, "Potassium is so yummy. Thank you. We appreciate your kindness and generosity. By the way, what's your name?"

"No problem," said the man. "My name is Timo."
He smiled – he was happy to see that the children liked his food and he was equally as glad that he was able to help them.

"You need to stay hydrated in this hot sun. By the way, what are you doing here anyway?" he wondered.

"We want to help clean up the beaches," explained Zedalla. "There's way too much plastic everywhere and when it ends up in the oceans, it's killing the animals."

Timo nodded. "Yes, yes!" he said, "There is too much plastic in the ocean. There is too much plastic on the beach. There is even plastic in our seafood! It is not good for people or animals. I don't use plastic. I use paper for my drinks and snacks. Single-use plastic is not allowed on this island. It's true! It is banned here. "

"That's good!" said the friends. "We think that's a great idea! There should be some sort of penalty for using plastic, especially in irresponsible ways."

"We want to try to get rid of plastic bags, cups, straws, and other single-use plastic products from our school and our community," said Tess.

Zedalla updated Timo about the map they found, the garbage patches, and some of the clean-up initiatives that she knew about. She told him the story about the whale with plastic in its stomach.

Timo knew exactly what she was talking about. He was aware of the problems with plastics in the ocean. One day while he was working at his shop, he discovered a sea turtle that had washed up on the shore. Sadly, the sea turtle was caught in a fishing net, which was made of – you guessed it – plastic.

The sea turtle was still alive, luckily. However, the netting was wrapped around her neck and mouth, so she probably hadn't eaten for a very long time. Needless to say, Timo was very upset and worried.

Timo knew he had to move quickly and carefully to cut the net off the sea turtle. He ended up saving the turtle's life. Timo named her Mojo. He took care of her for a few days until she was strong enough and ready to go back into the ocean.

He was sad to say goodbye to Mojo but pushed her out to sea after giving her a big hug. He knew he would probably never see her again, but he also knew he'd made a huge difference in her life.

From that day on, Timo regularly collected trash from the beach whenever he saw it, and he vowed to use less plastic himself.

The friends were awed and saddened by his story at first, but then they were glad to hear that there was a happy ending. It was almost like fate had brought them to Timo. He shared their feelings about plastic, and animals.

Timo agreed to help them in any way he could. After all, he had already given them water and snacks. Timo pointed the friends in the right direction as they began the next part of their adventure.

"This is the right place," said Timo, pointing toward town and the X on the map. "In town, you will find the team from Project Plastic that cleans up plastic in the oceans. They take boats out on cleaning trips all the time."

"Wow. So that's what's at the X. No treasure, but just what we were looking for anyway," said Zedalla, "I wonder if we could go on a Project Plastic cleaning trip…"

"Yes, yes, I am sure you could," said Timo. "I have been on several cleaning trips before. They always welcome new volunteers. They need as much help as they can get. Plastic in the ocean is a big mess and every day it becomes a bigger and bigger mess. I am sure they would appreciate the help."

"Well, good," said Nick. "We are ready to work, especially now that we've had some water to hydrate and a snack to refuel." He flexed his arm muscles, just in case nobody had noticed how strong and able he was. The girls rolled their eyes.

"Let's get on with it," suggested Zedalla, "while we all have enough energy to help. And while Nick still has those muscles."

They thanked Timo again and again for his generosity. They shook hands, gave hugs, and Timo even sent them off with some extra snacks for later.

"We are lucky to have found you," said Olivia, "We really appreciate everything you've done for us. Thanks!"

"Actually… do you want to come with us?" added Olivia. She was always thinking of others. She never wanted anyone to feel left out.

The others thought that was a good idea, too. They nodded to show Timo that they agreed and eagerly awaited his answer.

"No, no, no," said Timo, shaking his head and waving his hand. "I must stay here. I must keep my shop open. It is my livelihood. It is how I earn money to live. I'm sorry but I cannot go with you."

Timo invited the children to stop back anytime. Then they hoisted their backpacks onto their shoulders and headed down the path in the direction that Timo had showed them.

"We are so lucky!" said Tess. "Timo is pretty amazing. And kind. And generous."

"I wish he could come with us. He reminds me of, like, a wise, old uncle or something. And he knows the island like the back of his hand," said Nick.

"How well does he know the back of his hand?" asked Zedalla, teasing Nick like she often did.

Nick squinted. "Actually, I'm not really sure." He looked at the back of his own hand. "Come to think of it, I should probably get to know the back of my hand a little better."

With that, he started talking to his hand as if they just met.

"You're silly," said Zedalla.

They headed up the path, stopping to smell the purple hibiscus along the way. They waved to the birds and listened to the sounds of the island as they walked. They were energized and enthusiastic about what might happen next.

Chapter 9
Smells Like Chocolate

At the top of a hill, they referred to the map. It showed that they had to go around a koi pond, through a small farm, and over a bridge. If they followed that route, they would arrive in the 'little downtown' area of the island.

"Almost there," said Tess. "This is getting exciting! I can't wait to start helping!"

"Me, too. This is going to be awesome!" said Olivia.

"We are going to make a difference," said Zedalla.

"We already are!" said Nick. "I must say, we're pretty darn great, aren't we?"

"Indeed!" said the girls, holding their heads high with pride as they walked along.

The children found the pond and peered into the beautiful, blue water. The sun glistened off the surface. Between the sparkles, they could see koi fish swimming.

They watched the black, white and orange fish dart back and forth for several minutes.

"Hello, fishy, fishy," said Olivia. "Oh, they are so pretty. Look at all the different colors and spots. I wish I had a pond like this at my house. Maybe my goldfish, Benny, would like some big brothers and sisters."

"I could watch this all day," said Nick. He was completely mesmerized.

"No, you can't," said Zedalla, "We are on a mission, remember? Let's go."

They continued around the pond and came to a small farm.

"I wonder what they are growing here in this field," said Tess. "I know Hawaii is known for cocoa and chocolate, as well as other exotic fruits and plants, like pineapples and coconuts. However, I have never seen this kind of leaf or seed pod before."

She looked closer then gently touched one of the leaves on the tree. Tess was always sure to be respectful of other people's property, especially anything in nature.

They all looked closer. The red, orange, and yellow fruits hung from the trees. Each fruit was oblong, with ridges and small bumps.

"What in the world is that?" asked Olivia. "I have never seen anything like it before. It's so weird."

"It smells like chocolate!" shouted Zedalla, sticking her nose closer for a whiff.

"No way. That is not chocolate." said Nick. "I have never in my life seen red, orange, or yellow chocolate. Brown chocolate, sure. White chocolate, okay. But never colored chocolate, unless it's candy coated!"

"I don't know," said Tess. "I think Zedalla might be right. Tropical places often have plants that would never grow where we live."

When they got to the edge of the property, they saw a sign: Garden Island Chocolate Farm. .Zedalla and Tess were right. It was a chocolate farm. Those weird red and orange plants were cocoa plants. Inside the unusual pods, there were handfuls of cocoa beans that would eventually become chocolate.

A Hawaiian couple spotted them and motioned for them to come closer. The man and woman introduced themselves as the owners of the farm – Mr. and Mrs. Po. They smiled and spoke quickly to explain that they had lived on the island forever and only recently acquired the farm from Mr. Po's parents.

"Is it true you grow cocoa and chocolate here and then make it into candy bars and other chocolate stuff?" asked Nick.

"Totally true," said Mrs. Po. "Come on into our little shop and we'll give you a sample."

They followed the woman inside and were overwhelmed with the smell of fresh sweet chocolate, with a side of coffee. They found out later that it was also a coffee bean farm.

"My olfactory organs are loving this!" said Tess, taking in a huge sniff.

Nick rolled his eyes at Tess and said, "Tess, let me explain something to you. Some of us – actually, most of us – call this a 'nose'. Can you say 'nose'?"

Tess playfully rolled her eyes, but she got Nick's point.

Mr. Po gave each of the kids a sample of their top-selling, flavored chocolates and explained, "All of our cocoa is 100% Hawaiian made and grown. The volcanic soil, the regular rainfall, and the tropical sun help grow cacao plants with a unique flavor.

70

Tess smirked. She knew she was right about the rainfall and the sun. But she was pleased to learn that the volcanic soil was also necessary for growing all kinds of plants on the Hawaiian Islands.

"Mmm... blueberries!" said Zedalla. "SO good!"

Olivia tried one with mango flavor. "I never thought I would like mango chocolate. And it doesn't taste anything like any chocolate I've ever had, but I've gotta say – it's delicious."

"Well, let's be honest, you will eat practically anything," said Zedalla. "And you are always hungry, so it makes sense you would like it."

"Guilty," agreed Olivia, raising her hand.

Nick noticed a window to the left of the counter. Through it, he could see big machines and flying beans. They all ran to the window for a closer look.

"That's our little flinger factory," explained Mrs. Po with a giggle.

Mr. Po pointed to the machine and said, "First, we pick the cocoa pods, then we separate and sort the cocoa beans. Then we roast the beans to dry them. After that, the beans go through our custom-designed machine, which my son named 'the flinger.' It removes the shells and leaves the pure chocolate nib."

"What do you do with the nib?" asked Olivia.

Mr. Po continued, "People buy the nibs for cooking or baking different recipes. Some of the nibs get turned into chocolate paste."

Mrs. Po chimed in with excitement, "This is my favorite part." She clapped her hands with joy as she continued.

"After we make the paste, we add cocoa butter, sugar, vanilla, or milk powder. It all depends on whether we are making a batch of dark chocolate or milk chocolate. It is a long process of adding different ingredients and flavors, but eventually, we put the liquid chocolate mix into molds to make bars or other shapes."

"As you can tell, the long process is totally worth it!" added Mr. Po.

"So, how are the plants different from the cocoa plants? Is the process of making coffee the same?" asked Zedalla.

"Well, it's sort of similar," said Mrs. Po. "The plants look a little bit alike, and we have to separate the beans from the plant. We sun-dry the beans and then we roast them. Sometimes, we grind up the coffee beans to sell. Other times, people just buy the beans."

72

Zedalla noticed that Nick was fidgeting. He was tapping his foot and shaking his hand.

"Are you okay?" she asked.

"Yes. Great. Never better. Fine. Better than fine. 100%. Actually 200%. I just got a burst of energy. I feel like I could run a marathon, or, better yet, I could clean tons of plastic out of the whole ocean... or something," chattered Nick without stopping to take a breath.

Mrs. Po knew what had happened. "Oops. How much chocolate did you eat?" she asked. "I should have mentioned that the cocoa content is 80% in these bars. It is very strong and has some caffeine in it. I'm sorry. I should have told you to only eat a small amount at a time."

Nick continued to fidget and dance around. His eyes blinked fast and he was talking fast, too.

"That's okay. I ate the whole thing. It was so good. But, I'll be fine. Just moving a little fast at the moment. No big deal. Energizer bunny speed," continued Nick.

Zedalla smiled and said, "I think we should move on before he eats any more chocolate."

Tess and Olivia agreed, especially since they weren't exactly sure how long it would take to get where they were going.

The Po couple was familiar with Project Plastic, so Mrs. Po pointed them in the direction of a rickety bridge they had to cross to get to the downtown area. It was wooden with rope railings. It hung about 30 feet over a fast-rushing stream below.

"Cross the bridge and you will be in downtown. Just ask someone to show you where to find Project Plastic. Anyone will be happy to help you."

They thanked Mr. and Mrs. Po for their kindness, their information, and, of course, the chocolate.

After they crossed the bridge, the friends caught a glimpse of the small town up ahead. They saw people, shops, cars, and a lot more activity than they had seen since they arrived on the beach.

In one sense, they hated to leave the peace and quiet of natural Hawaii. But, in another sense, it was a relief to be near civilization. At least, they weren't on some abandoned island in the middle of nowhere.

Chapter 10
Little Downtown

They walked toward the busy area and sat on a park bench to review the map again. There were no street names or numbers, so they had to figure out where they were in reference to the other things on the map.

"I see a café-diner-restaurant-place over there," said Olivia.

"You *would* notice where they sell food," Zedalla teased. "And there's a pharmacy over there." She pointed to another building.

"Okay. So, where is the water clean-up crew building?" wondered Tess, looking around.

Nick was too busy watching some kids playing soccer in the street and he wasn't really paying attention.

"Hello!? We could use your help," said Zedalla, gently poking Nick in the ribs with her elbow.

"Ow!" he said, even though it didn't really hurt. "Okay, okay, I'll help."

He looked around and noticed lots of people walking up and down the sidewalk. He spotted a blond-haired woman wearing a bright blue T-shirt. She looked different from most of the other locals on the island. Most people in Hawaii had dark hair.

Nick also noticed that her shirt said "CREW" on the back and there was a picture of a swirly wave logo on the front. She was tan, as if she had been out in the sun for a while. She wore a hat and was carrying a big box with the label "Project Plastic." Without pointing, Nick told his friends what he saw.

"Hey, you guys, we could ask her. She looks like she knows about water and plastic," he said.

"Awesome. Now you're being helpful," teased Zedalla. "Let's go ask her."

The friends jumped up and hustled toward the woman. When she saw them rushing toward her, she was a little startled.

"Excuse me, maybe you can help us," began Zedalla. "We're looking for the water, plastic, clean-up team. The group that helps get plastic out of the oceans and saves animals and stuff.

We want to help, so do you know anything about that?"

"Are you asking about Project Plastic? Do you want to be part of the clean-up team?"

The friends nodded at the same time.

"Why don't you come with me to headquarters and maybe we can have you guys help with a clean-up. We have one scheduled for later today," suggested the woman.

"That's cool," said Nick. "What's your name?"

"I'm Angela," she replied. "I'm a volunteer for Project Plastic and I'm a vet here on the island."

"Aw. We love animals," said Olivia. "That's such a cool job. I dream about becoming a vet when I grow up. I have so many pets already and I just love taking care of them. I'd show you pictures, but my phone is dead."

"That's awesome!" said Angela, "We always need more people that love animals and know how to take care of them. It's a lot of hard work and sometimes it's sad to see animals hurting, but when you're able to help them it's super rewarding."

"Where's your office?" wondered Tess.

Angela said, "I just have a tiny office on the next block.

It's not much, but it's all I really need. Plus, I have a Jeep that I can take to different parts of the island. That way I can help animals in the wild or at their owner's homes. It's easier on the animals and their owners. I make a lot of house calls."

As they started walking, Nick offered to help Angela carry the box she was holding.

"What a gentleman you are!" said Angela. "Thanks, but I got it. It's not that heavy, so it's no big deal. It's a shipping box of our latest bracelets made from recovered ocean plastic. When people donate money to Project Plastic, we send them one of these bracelets." Angela showed them the bracelets. "They are very colorful and each one is 100% unique. They are very durable, since plastic lasts forever."

She gave each one of the kids a bracelet. "If you are going to be helping us, you might as well have one of these," she said. "All volunteers get one."

"Cool! What a great idea!" said Tess, admiring her new jewelry. "Aww, a little turtle! You guys! It's Mojo!"

"This will help me remember that I made the plastic pact," said Olivia.

"Exactly," agreed Zedalla. "When I see this bracelet, I'll think about the plastic problem and what I can do to help fix it."

78

"You know what? It would be so great if we could get our friends at school to donate to Project Plastic. Then they'd get to wear these bracelets, too. Then no one would ever forget how important this is," suggested Nick.

"That would be great," said Angela. "Follow me. I'll take you to Project Plastic headquarters."

They talked and walked through the center of town. They passed a man selling coconut water ice cream in ten different flavors. They passed a wishing fountain filled with pennies and coins. And they even passed street vendors selling leis, sunscreen, umbrellas, and lots of island-themed trinkets.

Finally, they reached a simple, one-story, cement building at the edge of town. The outside was light blue and there were some small windows near the roof.

A small sign on the front read: Project Plastic Headquarters. There was a door propped open with a milk crate that led inside.

Chapter 11
Project Plastic

"Come on in," she said. "Don't mind the mess. We are about to head out on our next clean-up, so things are kind of crazy at the moment."

Once inside, they saw one large room that was painted with the same blue color as Angela's T-shirt. The name Project Plastic was painted on one wall and below it was the logo. It was a swirl that looked like a curling wave and a few drops of splashing water. There was no sign of plastic in the logo, but that was on purpose. After all, there shouldn't be any plastic in the ocean, so the logo was just water.

"Woah!" said Nick, looking around, "This is so cool!"

To the left, there were a few desks and tables set up. One table had stacks of blue T-shirts like the one Angela was wearing. Another table had boxes with the Project Plastic logo on them.

Behind the tables were tall shelves stacked with different kinds of water gear – goggles, wet suits, flippers, nets, and other random equipment.

On the far side of the room, there was an open entryway to a small kitchenette. It had the typical necessities: a fridge, a sink, a table, and a shelf full of island snacks. A basket of fresh island fruit sat on the counter.

The whole room smelled like coconut-scented suntan lotion and coffee. Not a bad combination. It was clean and bright, with a few windows near the ceiling that let in plenty of sunlight.

A door at the other end of the building was also propped open and created a nice cross-breeze with the door where they came in. The room had an energetic and happy vibe.

A dozen people were busy doing different things, but they weren't too busy to greet the newcomers. Nobody stopped what they were doing, but each person in the room nodded, waved, or smiled at them, and they instantly felt welcome.

"Everyone here seems so nice!" said Zedalla.

"Everyone here is super nice," said Angela. "We are really lucky to have so many great volunteers."

The volunteers included women and men, young people and older people, different races – all different types of people.

They looked different, but they had one thing in common: they were all wearing the same blue shirts. Actually, two things in common: they were all dedicated to eliminating plastic in the oceans, too. A small group of people were sorting T-shirts and filling mailers with bracelets.

Angela explained, "Welcome to Project Plastic. This is where we process donations, coordinate the clean-up missions, and send out donor information and gifts. Most of these people are volunteers and we get new volunteers all the time. Everyone believes in this mission. We're lucky to have very talented people on our team. There is always work to do, so we can always use more hands. We're growing and expanding all the time. We will need to have a second place soon."

Angela introduced them to one of the workers sorting T-shirts, "Sarah, can you help find T-shirts for our newest helpers?"

"Absolutely," beamed Sarah, with a smile.

She handed each of the kids a T-shirt and said, "Put these on so everyone knows you are part of the team. Thanks for volunteering!"

They were official crew members on the clean-up team! They thanked Sarah and put the shirts on right over their regular clothes. They were ready.

Then Angela took them to a map on the wall and said, "The star shows where we are right now, here at headquarters. We are on one of the smaller, northernmost islands, which is part of Hawaii. This big blob is the Great Pacific Garbage Patch, also known as the GPGP."

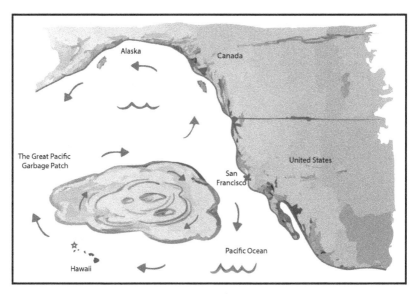

"Oh, I read about the GPGP," said Zedalla. "There's something like eight million tons of plastic and it's located only about 575 miles from the coast of California."

"You're correct," continued Angela.

"When we venture out on a clean-up mission, our little crew can only handle so much. We work mainly around the southern, outer edge of the GPGP. Luckily, there are lots of other groups working on this, too. Some of the bigger organizations have a lot more moneyto spend on crews and research. They also have some really amazing technology."

Angela called to one of the other workers, "Hey, John, can you help us for a minute? John is our resident expert on the latest ocean clean-up technology. He can tell you more about what the big organizations are working on."

Chapter 12
Captain John – Tech Expert

John introduced himself and welcomed them. Then he jumped right into a full explanation of the science behind the ocean clean-up technology.

"I have been following the Ocean Cleanup Project for a while, and they have some great initiatives. They just rolled out their newest army of systems that will clean up half of the GPGP in five years!" said John.

"Wow! How will they do it?" wondered Tess.

John continued, "Some scientists came up with a genius solution. Since larger plastic floats near the top of the water, they invented a giant, deep, slow-moving screen. Imagine a huge floating system – like a pool noodle – that is attached to an underwater screen – like a skirt.

"Interesting," said Zedalla.

"What about boats and tankers that need to pass through the ocean. Won't they destroy the screen invention with their motors and stuff?" asked Nick.

"Good question," said John. "The ships know where the floating screens are, so they just navigate around them. There should never be a problem."

"What about the ocean animals? Don't they get stuck in the screen thing?" wondered Zedalla.

"Get this. Ocean animals can swim under it, so they stay safe," replied John.

Olivia asked, "But don't the animals get stuck in the plastic that's in the water? We met a guy named Timo who saved a turtle from a fishing net."

John frowned. "Sadly, that part is true. Almost half of what the screen picks up is fishing gear that has been abandoned in the ocean – nets and other items. We are trying to get fishing boats to be more responsible for their equipment."

"Wow. I've never heard of anything like these floating screens. How did they come up with this idea in the first place?" Zedalla was both fascinated and curious.

"Another great question. The screen is a totally new idea. The organization launched this technology two years ago. Before that, scientists completed years of research. They tried all different methods until they determined that the screen idea was the most effective," said John.

"Is it working so far?" wondered Tess.

"Basically, yes," said John. "The idea is still in the early stages, so researchers are busy monitoring and updating all the time. Their goal is to clear 90% of the ocean's plastics within 20 years. So far, so good."

"That would be so awesome if they could get rid of that much trash! But, how do they know if the screen thing is working? I mean, if it's like a machine, then how do they know if it is picking up the garbage or not?" asked Tess.

John had an answer for that, too. "Each system is equipped with the latest technology. There are sensors, hi-tech cameras, lanterns, satellite pods, GPS systems navigation pods, and so on. That way, scientists can track and record information about where, when, and how much plastic is picked up."

Olivia was trying to follow the conversation, but admitted she was a little lost, "I can't even imagine what these things look like. They must be big, but I can't really picture what the system-thing is, or what the screen looks like. It's over my head."

"Let me show you," said John. He grabbed a binder from the table and opened it.

"This is what the invention looks like from the side. The floating part is at the top. Here it looks like a balloon, but in reality, it's curved like a pool noodle. The part below the water is the hanging screen. Those little bits are pieces of plastic."

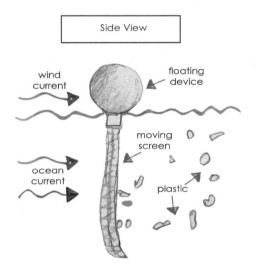

He flipped to the next page.

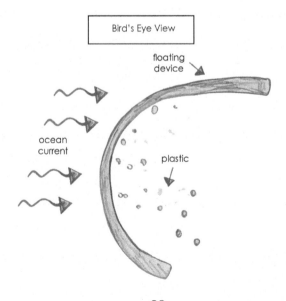

"And, this is what the technology looks like from above, like if you were in an airplane in the sky. The C-shaped thing you see is the floating device and the screen hangs in the water below it. The arrows show how the ocean currents naturally push the floating system to collect the pieces of plastic."

Nick was curious. "I bet that kind of technology costs millions of dollars. I wonder how they pay for it. I mean, who pays for it?"

John had an answer for everything. "Government agencies and different companies donate money to fund the project. Here's the really cool (and free) part. The ocean waves naturally move the system. Any extra equipment needed (like lights or cameras) is solar- powered."

"Okay. Still catching up right here." Olivia raised her hand. "Question. What does 'solar' mean?"

John explained, "Solar means it uses the power of the sun. Solar means sun. That kind of power will always be available and basically free, even on a cloudy day!"

Olivia nodded. "Ah-ha. That makes sense. Now that you mention it, we have some solar lights at home that are powered by the sun. I should have remembered that."

Now Zedalla had a question, "Okay, what do they do with the garbage once it is in the screen?"

"You guys are asking the best questions!" exclaimed John. "There is an ocean garbage boat that collects the trash every couple of months. The boat takes the trash to land, where it gets sorted and recycled."

Zedalla was in awe. "Wow! That is amazing. I never would have thought of something like that. Where do people come up with this stuff?"

John replied, "It's interesting because some people see a need, or a problem, and they want to fix it. They brainstorm a bunch of ideas, they experiment, and they learn from trying different things. There is always a way to solve a problem; you have to experiment until you find something that works."

Nick knew exactly what John was talking about, "That's what we do in science. We experiment with different methods. Sometimes they work and sometimes – EPIC FAIL. Our teacher has us record our findings then we change things and try again."

"Exactly," said John. "You are already practicing scientific methods! Now, if you'll excuse me, I must get ready for this trip. We leave in 20 minutes…"

Angela interrupted, "I'm not sure if he told you, but in addition to being a whiz about technology, John is also the captain of the ship."

"Wow! You mean, I just met a real live captain?" said Nick.

With that, he brought his feet together, stood up straight and tall, and saluted John.

"Aye, Aye, Captain," said Nick.

With a chuckle and a salute back, Captain John ducked out the back door. They peeked out after him. He walked to the edge of the pier and inspected the outside of the boat. Then he checked the gas level, the oil level, and made sure all the systems were in working order. He even checked the horn.

"Yep, horn works!" said Nick, covering his ears. "But now my ears don't work."

"I guess that means the boat is ready," said Zedalla. She could barely contain her excitement.

"What? What? I can't hear you," said Nick, cupping his ear and leaning toward Zedalla.

"Never mind," giggled Zedalla.

Chapter 13
The Mission

"Fifteen minutes until departure!" Angela called.

As she darted around the office, the whole team moved faster, and the room got louder and busier. More volunteers poured into the room with their blue shirts. Each volunteer signed the check-in clipboard, then walked out the back door – the same way Captain John had gone.

Angela called to Zedalla and her friends, "Please sign-in, too. Then follow the others out that back door. Christina will meet you at the end of the pier and she will tell you what to do next. See you on board!

They were very excited and a little nervous. They had never done anything quite like this before, but they knew they were making a difference. They scribbled their names on the sign-in sheet and headed down the pier. Zedalla skipped ahead of the others.

She sang a little tune she made up as she went:

"Project Plastic is now in motion, yeah, yeah!
We are going to clean the ocean, yeah, yeah!
Pick up trash, we're on a mission, yeah yeah!
Time to work, no time for fishin', yeah, yeah!"

The boat wasn't huge, but it wasn't dinky either. It was somewhere in between. It was about 50 feet long, rather narrow, and had a Captain's perch up front. They saw Captain John as they approached.

The outside of the boat was gray, and the inside was white. It was clean and the sun bounced off the metal poles and rails. On the side of the boat was the name of the ship: Holoi Moana. In Hawaiian, that meant "Clean Ocean."

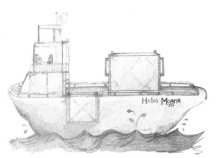

When they got to the boarding ramp, Christina greeted them with a smile.

"Hi, guys!" she said, "Welcome aboard! It's great to have you as volunteers for Project Plastic. On the hooks over there, you can choose a life jacket – the smaller ones are near the bottom. Put it on and fasten it so it's nice and snug. Everyone must wear one on the boat at all times. Then grab a net from the shelf and find a place to sit."

93

They followed Christina's orders and put on their life jackets.

A bench extended all the way around the edge of the boat. It was the perfect design because each person could easily reach his or her net into the water. In the center of the boat, there was a large, empty metal bin.

Olivia squirmed a little, she had buckled her jacket too tight. Nick put his net on his head so he could help adjust her buckles with both hands.

"You look ridiculous," giggled Olivia. "But I do appreciate your help."

Tess peered over the edge into the shallow water and sand below. The water was so clear that she could see some shells and fish swimming around near the bottom.

Other people climbed aboard, put on their life jackets, and grabbed their nets. The boat filled up fast with about 20 volunteers. Once everyone was aboard and seated, Christina and Angela introduced themselves and said a few words.

Angela began, "Hello everybody! Welcome to Project Plastic: Mission Six!" Everyone on the boat cheered and clapped.

Once everyone quieted again, Angela continued, "We are so pleased that you could join us on this ocean clean-up trip!

As you know, it is a very important job and we thank you for your dedication. Today we are going to navigate near the GPGP and collect as much trash as we can. We hope to fill the bin in the center of the boat, which holds about 5,000 gallons."

Christina added, "Thanks for being here. I want to go over a few rules for the boat, so we ensure that all volunteers are safe.

"First, you must keep your life jacket on at all times. The weather is supposed to be perfect and the waves should be calm, but the waters can get very deep. We don't want anyone to fall in, and we want to ensure that everyone stays safe – no matter what.

"Second, when you are standing to collect trash in your net, please do not lean over to grab something that is out of reach. Please hold on to the metal railing that wraps around the boat with one hand, while you reach for trash with the net in your other hand."

Christina continued, "Angela is going to pass out gloves so that nobody has to touch the nasty trash. Keep in mind that the garbage has been in the ocean and may have germs, parasites, or even chemicals on it. Please use the gloves to keep yourself safe."

"Wait, aren't these gloves made of plastic?" asked Tess. "Doesn't that kind of defeat the purpose of picking up plastic trash, then adding to the plastic problem with the gloves?"

"You might think so," answered Christina,

"but these gloves are different. They're made from natural latex, which is harvested from the Hevea Brasiliensis Tree. Therefore, they are natural, safe, and 100% biodegradable."

"100% bio-huh?" wondered Olivia.

Christina repeated, "Biodegradable. The gloves are made from natural – biological –ingredients, so they will naturally decay. They won't stay around forever, like human-made plastics that contain chemicals."

Olivia nodded in surprised agreement that biodegradable was a good thing. Angela passed out the gloves.

Nick pulled and snapped his gloves like a doctor as he adjusted them. "Ouch," he whispered.

Then Angela said, "Once you collect trash in your net, some volunteers will walk around to collect it in these big blue bags and then throw them in the metal bin when the bag is full." She held one up.

"Wait, we're using plastic bags to pick up plastic… " Zedalla whispered. She squinted and hesitated. It didn't make sense.

Angela must have heard Zedalla because she explained, "These bags are not made of plastic. They're made from vegetable starch, so they're eco-friendly, and biodegradable, like the gloves."

Zedalla and Tess each gave a thumbs up.

"We have a medic on board if anyone feels sick." She pointed to a female near the back, and explained, "Charlie will be happy to help you if you need any medical attention."

"Does anyone have any questions?" asked Angela, pausing briefly see if anyone had questions, then continued, "Okay, then we are ready to go!"

She turned and gave the thumbs up signal to Captain John, who was at the front of the boat. He waved to the volunteers and everyone waved back.

Captain John started the engine and carefully pulled out of the harbor. The boat moved slowly at first, until they were out of the busy marina. The warm breeze felt nice on Zedalla's face and hair. She closed her eyes and enjoyed the ride.

Chapter 14
A Boatload of Garbage

As the boat picked up speed, everyone held on to the railing, just in case. The friends enjoyed the occasional bump over small waves and the light spray of cool water.

Every once in a while, Tess yelped when she wasn't expecting the splash. The warm Hawaiian air dried everything quickly, so the ride was quite pleasant.

Zedalla looked north, south, east, and west. She saw nothing but ocean water in every direction. It was bright blue, and the sun danced on the waves. Beautiful! *So, this is the Pacific Ocean,* she thought to herself. She couldn't imagine the nastiness of the garbage patch when her current view was so amazing.

This water was very different from the murky water of Lake Michigan she was used to. She loved swimming in the lake, but the water wasn't nearly this clear and blue. The sand wasn't nearly as soft either. Plus, the sun was never this bright.

For miles and miles, the boat kept a steady pace and bobbed up and down. After about 30 minutes, Captain John slowed to a crawl. It was very slow, but it was the perfect speed for reaching trash in the ocean without falling in.

"Okay, crew. Hold on to the railing and get your nets in the water," said Christina.

"Are we near the GPGP?" asked Zedalla.

"Yep, we are at the southern edge of the GPGP. We'd have to travel another five hours east to get to the center of the garbage patch. We would be overwhelmed with trash. Since we are a small operation, we stay on the outer ring. There is still plenty of trash here."

"Wait, we would have to go five more *hours* to get to the center of garbage!", exclaimed Olivia. "When we drive three hours to get to my grandparent's house that feels like a really long way and that's to go somewhere fun. It makes me feel bad that ocean animals have to live with that much garbage."

"It makes me feel bad, too," agreed Zedalla. "And actually, a little mad. We need to make this better for our ocean friends. Let's get to work!"

Now they felt even more inspired to work hard. They held on to the railing while dropped their nets into the water. Right away, the nets caught some trash.

"I caught a water bottle and a straw," said Tess. "Grrr. Single-use plastic," she scowled.

"I got a couple plastic bags," said Olivia. "I'm not surprised. I see these awful bags everywhere! In the lake, blowing down the street, stuck in trees, wrapped around bushes. That's crazy! Why don't people just throw the bags away where they belong? Or recycle them? Or reuse them? For example, I use them for my cat's litter. Ugh. Okay, rant over."

"I don't know what the heck I got, but it's definitely disgusting," said Nick, holding up his net with something stringy, slimy, and muddy hanging from it. "Actually, I prefer not to know what this is." He made a fake puking sound.

"Ew," said Zedalla, backing away. "That is SO gross. Do not, I repeat, DO NOT come near me with that, that, that – whatever that nastiness is."

Zedalla picked up some random wrappers and trash, and the other volunteers helped collect everything in the big blue bags. Once a bag was full, they tied it and hurled it over the top of the metal bin in the center of the boat. It looked like a giant dumpster, but it didn't really smell like one. At least, not yet.

The crew worked and worked while the boat moved slowly through the water.

"I can't believe we are a thousand miles away from the GPGP center and there is still so much trash!" exclaimed Zedalla. "It's kind of ridiculous!"

"That just goes to show you how much trash is in the ocean," said Tess. "I agree with Olivia, it's really pretty sad."

Olivia said, "And, the really scary thing is that it gets filled up with plastic again after people clean it."

Nick put in his two cents, "I can't believe how much broken-down plastic has already hurt the oceans, the environment, and so many animals we don't even know about. And us, for that matter!"

Angela heard the kids talking. "This is our sixth mission. Each time we clean, we fill that metal bin. Basically, we're just maintaining our little job of clearing one space. People continue to use plastic and it often ends up in the oceans. We're just trying to catch up each time we do a clean-up."

Zedalla was thinking out loud, "It seems like we really have to stop the problem at its source – I mean, the way people use plastic and then how they get rid of plastic."

"Exactly," said Angela.

"Lots of engineers, scientists, and research groups are working on alternatives to plastic packaging, utensils, wrappers, and things like straws and bags. We aren't experts when it comes to that stuff."

"Instead, we try to keep the oceans clean for the animals and the environment. To help in other ways, we are thoughtful about the products we use, we try to eliminate single-use plastic, and we support companies that make quality changes for the future."

Zedalla said, "I think it's great that you are doing what you do. Every little bit helps, even if it doesn't seem like it. The whole plastic problem is overwhelming. We promise to use less plastic, but that's a hard change to make. For example, I'm thirsty, and yet, I don't have a water bottle, which would be really great right now."

"Funny you should mention that," said Angela. "We just discovered an invention to solve that exact problem."

She walked to a cooler in the corner and opened it. Inside were clear balls filled with water. She held one up to show the kids.

"This is a water ball," she said. "You can put the whole thing in your mouth and drink it. No plastic waste."
"Wait, what? Water ball? Oooh – You just blew my mind, Angela!" said Nick "Can we try one?"

"Absolutely," said Angela.
"The name of these water balls is Ohoo!"

102

She handed each child a water ball. They stared at them. They shook them. They even smelled them.

"This is amazing! Or should I say, AMAZEBALLS," exclaimed Zedalla. "I have never seen anything like this in my life! How do they… I mean how do they get like… What is this part on the outside?"

Zedalla was rambling in her excitement. She had all sorts of questions that filled her head at the same time, and she couldn't get them all out.

Angela wasn't really sure how to explain the water balls, but she tried, "I think the company freezes water then dips the ice ball into a natural mixture, like a tasteless seaweed extract. That coats the ice, which holds the water's shape when it melts. It's perfect to take on our excursions because there's no waste and people often get thirsty."

Nick put his water ball in his mouth. His eyes widened as he tasted then swallowed it.

"That was an adventure in my mouth," he said.

"Mmm. Squishy," said Tess.

"Tastes just like… water," said Olivia.

"That's the idea," said Zedalla.

Zedalla tried her water ball and said, "That is the weirdest thing I've ever eaten... or did I drink it? I don't even know."

Angela explained, "You know, some of these great ideas actually start with an experience like this one. People recognize a problem and want to solve it. They start thinking and brainstorming and come up with some great concepts that actually work. Every invention comes from some idea to solve a problem."

That comment really got the friends thinking.

"We're going to come up with something," said Zedalla, "I just know it."

"That's the spirit," said Angela, "You never know when a good idea will hit. It's always good to carry a notebook so you can keep track of ideas. You don't want to forget something important."

"Good thinking," said Zedalla. "Actually, I've had my notebook in my backpack this whole time, but I haven't taken any notes since we left the playground."

"Well, your hands are busy now, but you can jot down notes on the way back to headquarters. Good researchers and scientists reflect on their experiences. It helps you learn," said Angela.

"Believe it or not, we all do it. Then we share our notes and decide if we should change something about what we're doing. We always want to improve. Just something to think about."

"We will definitely do that," said Zedalla. "It's hard to remember everything in your head, especially when there's so much going on. I have to write things down or I will forget."

"Me too," said Nick, "But, if I write things down while I'm IN the experience, then I really wouldn't be experiencing the experience, and that wouldn't be good either."

"True," said Angela, "If you are present in the moment of an experience, then you'll likely remember details a little better."

"Okay. Well, back to work," said Christina. "We've got more trash to clean up. The metal bin is only about half full. Great job so far, everybody."

The crew kept working. They filled bags, they dumped bags, and they caught all kinds of trash in the nets. Straws. Bags. Bottles. Containers. Fishing wire. Wrappers. And plenty of who knows what.

A short time later, Christina climbed the little ladder and peeked into the metal bin.

"We're filling up the bin!" she said. "Keep up this pace and we should be full in about 20 minutes."

The friends kept working, filling their nets. Soon, trash was sticking out of the top of the metal bin. Christina and Angela stood up in front of the crew.

105

"We did it!" said Angela, "We filled the bin with 5,000 gallons of trash! That's awesome! Thanks for all your hard work! Give yourselves a round of applause."

Everyone clapped. Then the friends exchanged high-fives and a few pats on the back.

"We are pretty great, aren't we? It feels so good to be a part of this," said Zedalla proudly.

"I will collect the nets now and we will head back to headquarters," said Angela. "Feel free to rest your eyes on our way back, as I'm sure you're all tired from all that hard work."

Chapter 15
The Return

The ride back to the harbor seemed much faster than the ride out to sea. Maybe it was because everyone was tired from being in the sun and picking up trash. Zedalla slept most of the way, resting her head on Nick's shoulder while he dozed off, too.

Olivia and Tess were busy enjoying the scenery and the cool spray of mist on their faces. The ride was very relaxing.

In a matter of what seemed like minutes, the boat reached the harbor and slowed as it entered the no-wake zone. Anyone who had dozed off noticed the difference in speed and woke up. Once they made it to the dock, people stretched, yawned, and gathered their personal items. Angela stood up to say a few words.

"Attention please," she said. "We have arrived back at headquarters. I'm sorry to cut your nap short, but it's time to exit the boat. If you have any last bits of trash to be thrown away, please add them to the bin in the center of the boat."

She paused then continued, "We will have a meeting inside in about ten minutes and then you'll be free to go. Thank you all again for your time and efforts in getting plastic out of our oceans."

Eventually, the boat came to a stop and a few volunteers helped to secure the boat to the dock. Zedalla and her friends let the adult volunteers get off first. While they waited, they watched some fish enjoying their crystal blue home. They were glad they could help with Project Plastic. They were so zoned out that they hadn't noticed the boat and pier were empty.

Then, as they stood up to exit, the boat tipped back and forth, just gently enough to cause them to lose their balance. They grabbed onto each other's hands so they wouldn't fall to the floor.

At that exact moment, the sun bounced off the shiny hand railing and onto Zedalla's bracelet. Just as it had happened on the playground, the sunlight reflected onto each of their faces, nearly blinding them. And, the same colors lit the same faces as before.

"I think I know what's happening," said Zedalla.

"Thank goodness. We DO have a way home," said Nick.

"Let's hope so," said Olivia, crossing her fingers for luck.

"Grab hands and hold on tight. I hope the trip home is as safe, fast, and as easy as it was to get here," said Tess.

Suddenly the waves kicked up a little and the mist sprinkled onto their faces. The warm air moved faster and swirled around them. Olivia's hair was flying left and right again. A strange whizzing sound grew louder and louder. Dark clouds started to fill the sky and closed in around the sun. Before the sun disappeared completely, the light flashed again and bounced off the metal railing and onto Zedalla's bracelet.

They closed their eyes to avoid the bright light. With a loud pop, the whizzing sound stopped abruptly. The wind stopped, too. It was eerily quiet.

Slowly, they opened their eyes. They couldn't believe it, but they were also extremely relieved. They were back at the top of the playground tower where the whole adventure began.

"Holy cow!" said Nick, "That was SO crazy!"

"And super-fast, too!" said Zedalla. "It didn't even feel like we were gone."

Tess checked her hi-tech watch.
"Oh my gosh, you guys. This is so wild! We left the playground at 3:11, and right now, it is exactly 3:11. We are officially time travelers!"

Olivia couldn't believe what Tess was saying.

"Seriously!?!" she gasped. "Let me see that watch."

109

Tess was right, but Olivia still couldn't believe it.

"Well, I guess that's good. Our parents won't even be worried since we were gone for no time at all. And my cats will have no idea I was even gone."

"Good thing," said Zedalla. "I'm trying to think of what we need to do now. There is so much information swirling around in my head. I have all these ideas about how we could start at school. Ugh! It's too much."

"Well, Angela suggested that we reflect on our experiences and write notes about what we did, what we learned, and what we're thinking about. That's a good place to start," suggested Tess.

Nick agreed. "Yeah, I've got a lot swirling around in my brain, too. I definitely gotta get some of that out of my head. I think I'm going to go home, chill out a little bit, and then jot down some notes. Might be good if we all did the same. Then maybe we get together tomorrow and talk about what we're going to do next."

Everyone thought that sounded like a great idea.

"Plus, I'm like soooo hungry," said Olivia.

"Shocking," teased Zedalla.

With that, they hopped up, slid down the slide, and jumped off. At the bottom of the tower, they exchanged high fives.

Then they headed in the direction of their homes.

"Later, gators," said Olivia, heading down Carton Ave.

"After while, crocodile," said Nick, walking off with the girls in the other direction.

Zedalla and Tess left Nick off at the corner near his house.

"Toodle-oo, kangaroo," said Zedalla.

Nick was at a loss for how to respond, since he didn't want to use 'gator' or 'crocodile' again.

"Um, um...I got nothin'," he said. "My brain is completely fried," he sulked down the street toward his house. He was disappointed that he couldn't be funny at this very moment.

Zedalla and Tess giggled anyway and kept walking. Even when he wasn't trying to be funny, he was funny.

"Wow! That was one incredible adventure," said Zedalla.

"I know!" agreed Tess. "I still can't believe we were actually in Hawaii. And for literally no time at all. I feel like we accomplished so much though. I think we made a difference."

"Right?" agreed Zedalla. "It's amazing how much trash we collected in a short time.We did make a difference. I know we did.

I'm excited to think about what we can do at school and in the neighborhood."

Zedalla kept thinking out loud, "If we get everyone to realize how important it is, our little efforts could become really big. I can't rest until I can brainstorm a little bit."

"Do what you will, Zedalla," said Tess. "I am going to go home, flop onto my comfy couch, kick up my feet, and veg out for a while. That adventure took a lot out of me. See you later, friend." Tess gave Zedalla a hug and headed down the sidewalk to her house.

Finally, Zedalla reached her front steps. She climbed up, opened the door, dropped her book bag on the ground, and fell into the couch. Her mind was racing, but her body was not cooperating. She had to admit that she was pretty worn out, too.

Before she knew it, she was lightly snoring...

Chapter 16
Divide and Conquer

After a short cat nap, Zedalla woke to the sound of her mother's voice. "Hey, Z, how was your day? It must have been busy, because you never sleep like this. Are you feeling okay?"

Zedalla stretched her arms and let out a big, loud yawn. "Yeah. Actually, I feel great!" she said.

Suddenly she remembered her adventure, which at that very moment, she couldn't decide if it was a dream or real.

"Just had a busy day," she said. "We learned a ton and I'm just thinking about plastics in our oceans."

"Oh, you mean after the story on the news last night? Right. Well, I'm glad you're okay," said her mom. "I'd love to hear more about what you are learning over dinner. First, let me go change out of my work clothes, and then we can talk in a little bit. Okay?"

"Sure, Mom, that sounds good," said Zedalla.

Suddenly, Zedalla remembered that she had wanted to read the paper about the gems. She was so curious to see what the colors meant.

She ran upstairs to her room and found the red pouch with the paper. She opened the pouch and unrolled the paper. She read it. She reread it. Woah.

Synchronicity of Spirit

Passion

Empathy   Creativity

Wonderment

When the qualities are balanced and harmonious, magical things can happen.

She flipped the paper over and read about the gems and what they represented. Woah.

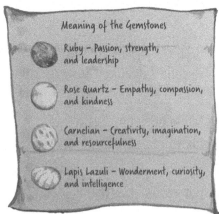

Meaning of the Gemstones

Ruby – Passion, strength, and leadership

Rose Quartz – Empathy, compassion, and kindness

Carnelian – Creativity, imagination, and resourcefulness

Lapis Lazuli – Wonderment, curiosity, and intelligence

Zedalla realized almost immediately that each stone clearly represented one of her friends.

114

She remembered when her friends were in the playground tower and the light bounced off the gems and onto each of their faces. She knew which friend's face matched which color, so the meaning and the color behind the gems made perfect sense.

Olivia's face had reflected a pink light. That was the color of the Rose Quartz stone, which represents Empathy. It was a perfect fit for Olivia – she was so caring, intuitive, and thoughtful, especially when it came to her family, friends, and animals.

Nick's face had reflected the deep orange light of the Carnelian gem. That stone represents Creativity. He was clever and silly, and often had great ideas. He was certainly a one-of-a-kind thinker with an amazing imagination.

And, Wonderment, the blue Lapis Lazuli gemstone, well that was Tess for sure. She wondered about everything. Her curiosity led her to get lost in books and all kinds of learning experiences. She absorbed information like a sponge, which made her a successful student, and a smart friend.

Not only was Zedalla drawn to the beauty of the bright red Ruby gem that represented Passion, but she also knew that represented her. She felt it.

Grandma G was always said things like, "I see that passion in your eyes, Z. Whatcha gonna do with all that passion, girl? Gotta do something with it."

Zedalla felt the energy and passion, but she didn't know exactly how it could help her or anyone else. This plastic pact initiative was something she felt strongly about. She was so motivated and energized by the idea of helping animals and the larger environment. She wanted to reduce single-use plastic and clean up her neighborhood. Maybe this is where it would all begin.

Zedalla concluded that she and her friends must have been in the right place at the right time on the playground tower. When they held hands and the sunlight bounced off the gemstones, that must have activated the magical power of the stones. And when the friends were all together, working cohesively to make the world better, the four gem qualities were balanced and in harmony. That's what brought about the magic.

Zedalla looked at the gem paper again. She thought she knew what the word 'synchronicity' meant, but she looked it up on her phone, just to be sure.

Synchronicity: Meaningful coincidences that do not appear to have any causal connections.

The same thing happened on the boat after the clean-up, which brought them back home.

Zedalla yawned again, but she was re-energized by the knowledge of the gemstones. She couldn't wait to share the details with her friends. But she didn't want to get stuck on the phone with each of them right now – she had work to do.

She picked up her notebook and the gel pen that had dropped to the floor when she dozed off.

She flipped to the first blank page and wrote, 'Project Plastic: Part 2' at the top. She jotted down a few things she remembered, and then doodled on the page while she thought some more.

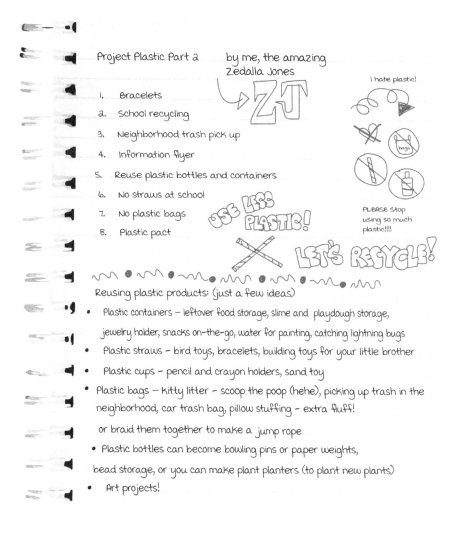

Project Plastic Part 2 by me, the amazing Zedalla Jones

I hate plastic!

1. Bracelets
2. School recycling
3. Neighborhood trash pick up
4. Information flyer
5. Reuse plastic bottles and containers
6. No straws at school
7. No plastic bags
8. Plastic pact

USE LESS PLASTIC!

PLEASE stop using so much plastic!!!!

LET'S RECYCLE!

Reusing plastic products: (just a few ideas)
- Plastic containers – leftover food storage, slime and playdough storage, jewelry holder, snacks on-the-go, water for painting, catching lightning bugs
- Plastic straws – bird toys, bracelets, building toys for your little brother
- Plastic cups – pencil and crayon holders, sand toy
- Plastic bags – kitty litter – scoop the poop (hehe), picking up trash in the neighborhood, car trash bag, pillow stuffing – extra fluff!
  or braid them together to make a jump rope
- Plastic bottles can become bowling pins or paper weights, bead storage, or you can make plant planters (to plant new plants)
- Art projects!

"Notes, notes, notes," said Zedalla, tapping her pen on her chin as she thought about what to write.

She turned the page in her notebook and wrote, 'Information for the Informational Flyer' at the top. Zedalla giggled when she realized how long the header was - because she had written a variation of the word 'information' twice

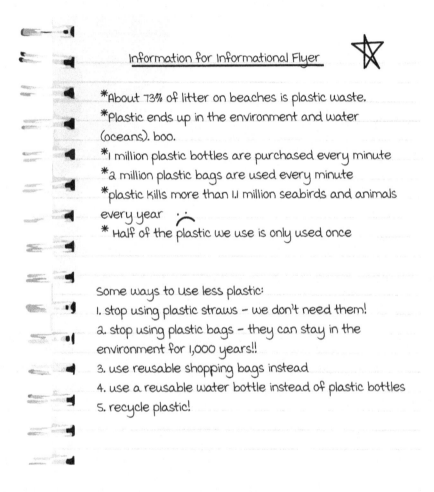

Information for Informational Flyer

*About 73% of litter on beaches is plastic waste.
*Plastic ends up in the environment and water (oceans). boo.
*1 million plastic bottles are purchased every minute
*2 million plastic bags are used every minute
*plastic kills more than 1.1 million seabirds and animals every year
* Half of the plastic we use is only used once

Some ways to use less plastic:
1. stop using plastic straws - we don't need them!
2. stop using plastic bags - they can stay in the environment for 1,000 years!!
3. use reusable shopping bags instead
4. use a reusable water bottle instead of plastic bottles
5. recycle plastic!

Zedalla continued searching the internet and took notes.

Eventually, she'd make it into a cool flyer, but for now, she just wanted to get her ideas out of her head and down on paper.

Meanwhile, Tess, Nick, and Olivia were busy jotting down their own notes about their experiences. The friends didn't know it, but separately, they had each written down some really interesting ideas to build on the trip. Each perspective was unique.

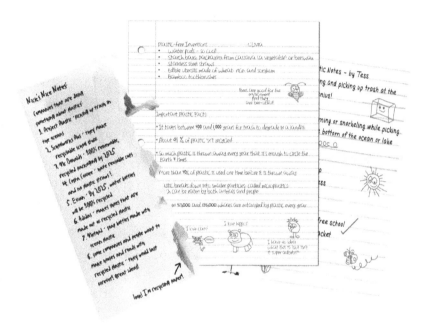

They would get the chance to share their great information with each other at the tower tomorrow. After a good effort of remembering and taking notes, they all packed up their notebooks (and Nick packed up his random envelope filled with notes - he was nothing if not resourceful) and they all turned in for the night.

Chapter 17
Taking Action!

The next day, the friends met up on their way to school as they normally did. They talked about their notes briefly, but they were still tired from their trip to the Great Pacific Garbage Patch. They agreed to meet up after school in the playground tower.

It was a long day. It was hard to focus. Zedalla was busy thinking about her flyer and what information she might have forgotten to include.

She doodled in her notebook. She drew a picture of her new bracelet from Project Plastic.

Then she drew a silly picture of Timo and Mojo, smiling as she remembered how kind Timo was to them.

During science, she realized that Miss Moore was one of the only teachers with a recycling bin in the classroom. She recycled paper and plastic. That was a good thing, but why didn't the other teachers recycle? Zedalla could only imagine how much paper was thrown away every day. *Ugh.*

At lunch, she noticed all the little plastic straws in little plastic wrappers. "Really? Do we really need straws for our milk?" she wondered.

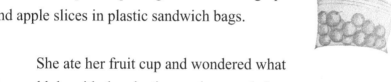

She watched her classmates eat chips and cookies from plastic packages. Others had grapes and apple slices in plastic sandwich bags.

She ate her fruit cup and wondered what she could do with the plastic cup that was left. What a waste.

Zedalla felt a little disgusted at the amount of plastic (and uneaten food) that was going into the garbage.

"Our school is so wasteful," she thought to herself. "This is out of control."

Zedalla tried to stay positive, but it was hard not to feel a little depressed over the enormity of the waste. Somehow, she made it through the day.

As soon as the bell rang, Zedalla and her friends ran outside and climbed to the top of the playground tower. They dropped their backpacks and sat in a circle.

"I thought the end of the day would never come," said Zedalla.

"Me neither!" shouted Nick, "It's so hard to concentrate on fractions and haiku poems when there are so many more important things going on in the world."

Olivia immediately opened her notebook. Then she grabbed a fruit snack bar from her backpack, because – of course – she was hungry. She nibbled on her snack while the others got settled.

Zedalla started the meeting by sharing some of her ideas. Then each of them said what they remembered about their trip. Then they described the new information they discovered. Between the four friends, they had a lot of information and just needed to decide how to move forward.

Tess had an idea. "My dad's always saying, 'attack the low-hanging fruit first.'"

"What? Low-hanging fruit? You mean, fight the bananas and apples? I don't get it. What in the world does that mean?" asked Nick.

Tess continued, "That means that you should do the things that are easiest first, before you move on to the big things. Like, for example, we could start a playground clean-up right here at our school. That would be super easy place to start."

"I agree. I think that's a logical place to begin. I don't think it would require much in the way of materials or preparation either," said Zedalla. "We could probably implement that pretty easily."

"I wonder if we should get permission from Mrs. Singer first," said Olivia.

"Good point," said Zedalla. "I imagine the principal would like to know what's going on."

"I am NOT talking to the principal," said Nick, who had experienced a few run-ins with Mrs. Singer.

He was clever, creative, and funny, but not always in the right place or at the right time. For example, Nick learned the hard way that cracking jokes in the middle of the school assembly was frowned upon and making faces at his friends during the fire drill were neither appropriate nor acceptable, at least according to Mrs. Singer.

Based on Nick's history, Zedalla knew she would have to lead the charge with Mrs. Singer, and she was fine with that.

"After the last bell, I'm going to go in there and see if I can just put a bug in her ear," she said.

Nick looked shocked. "What kind of bug are you putting in her ear?"

"Not a real bug," laughed Zedalla. "It's just an expression. I'm going to give her the idea and get her thinking about it."

Tess changed the subject, "Okay. Anyway, I found this other thing online about a school in England that became plastic-free. Apparently, you can write to them and request a package that guides you through the process of what to do to become a plastic-free school."

"That's awesome!" said Zedalla. "Do you want to send them a message and request the package?"

"Already done," said Tess proudly.

"Great!" said Zedalla. "That will really help us. So, let's start with the playground clean-up. Then maybe we can look at the plastic waste in the lunchroom next. It's atrocious."

Everybody agreed on the plan. The last bell rang. Zedalla gathered her things and headed back into the school building to find the principal. Olivia and Tess stood up, too.

Nick waited.. Zedalla gave him the look. He knew the look.

Reluctantly, he stood up and followed. Nick was often guilted into things by FOMO (fear of missing out). Then he thought that maybe this would change Mrs. Singer's mind about him. Who knows?

They went inside and asked the secretary if they could speak with Mrs. Singer. The principal heard them outside her office and motioned for them to enter.

"Come in," she called to them. "What's up?"

Mrs. Singer was young, friendly, and only a little intimidating. Most principals are – at least at some level. She liked to have a good connection with students. She was professional and kind. She could joke with students, but everyone knew when she meant business. That made her an effective principal.

Zedalla led her friends into the office. Nick shuffled in behind the others. Zedalla took the lead and explained what they were thinking and what they wanted to do. Mrs. Singer listened, nodding periodically.

When Zedalla paused, Mrs. Singer said, "Wow! You guys are really thinking positively about the environment. I like your ideas and I totally support what you're doing – 100%. We need to do something right away. Thanks for bringing this to my attention."

She paused for a moment and checked her desk calendar. She mumbled and pointed. She drew arrows, circled something, flipped to the next month. Finally, she said, "I think we should start this sooner rather than later. What if we set up a trash pick-up for Friday during each recess? That way, each of the classes will have a chance to help."

"Perfect!" exclaimed Zedalla, who was very pleased that it was much sooner than she had anticipated. Friday was only two days away!

Mrs. Singer jotted down some notes and said, "I will ask the custodian to supply you with a rolling garbage can and a large garbage bag. I will also ask him to provide a recycling bin for any bottles or cans that you find."

"That would be great!" said Zedalla.

"But how will we get the word out about the pick-up in such a short time? Friday is only two days away," asked Tess.

"Suggestion," said Mrs. Singer. "What if I gave you some time to describe the pick-up project on the announcements tomorrow morning?"

"Sure, I can do that," said Zedalla.

Mrs. Singer reminded Zedalla that she should complete a brief outline of what she planned to say. She should include information about who, what, where, when, why, and how the pick-up will take place.

"Come find me tomorrow morning so I can look over what you've written. You can go on right after my update. Now run along and I'll see you tomorrow," said Mrs. Singer.

The friends thanked Mrs. Singer for her time and support. She waved them out of her office, adding, "I can't wait to see a sparkling clean playground."

Olivia headed home one way and the others went off in the opposite direction. Nick and Tess talked about how excited they were that Mrs. Singer was on board with their project, and how quickly they got permission to move forward.

Zedalla was unusually quiet. She was busy planning what she was going to say on the announcements. At the corner, she stopped thinking long enough to wave to her friends.

When she got home, Zedalla prepared her speech. She wrote notes, key ideas, and bullet points. She reviewed and edited. Zedalla wondered if anybody would participate. She was hopeful. What could she say to get them excited about picking up trash? Maybe the right words would come to her when she needed them.

She rehearsed her speech as Mrs. Singer had suggested. She practiced in front of her bathroom mirror. She practiced over the phone during her nightly conversation with Tess, too. Tess thought it sounded good. As she went to bed that night, Zedalla felt ready. And she wasn't the least bit nervous.

ANNOUNCEMENT SPEECH

Who: you, me, everyone - we all need to keep our school clean!
What: It's a playground trash pick-up
Where: The playground
When: Friday during each recess
Why:
1. because we should have a clean playground,
2. because litter is ugly to look at,
3. because trash can end up in the oceans where it can hurt animals and sometimes, even people.

How: We want to use human power of all students at our school - we will have a large garbage can and a recycling can. You can put your trash in there.

Other important things to say:
- A whale in the ocean hand tons of plastic in its stomach. It almost died! (didn't it die?)
- Animals eat plastic because they think its food.
- Animals die every day because of human trash.
- Researchers think there is more trash in the oceans than there are animals.
- Plastic does not ever disappear. It stays in the environment forever (at least for a long, long, long, long time).

Chapter 18
Announcing – Playground Pick-Up

On Thursday morning, the friends met up on the playground as usual, and Zedalla shared her speech with them. They all approved.

Then Zedalla reported to the school office in plenty of time before the announcements. She sat in the chair outside Mrs. Singer's office and practiced her speech again.

Miss Boyer, the school nurse, found Zedalla sitting there and said, "I heard about your project! I think it's great! I'd like to donate some eco-friendly gloves for you to use."

"That would be awesome!" exclaimed Zedalla. "I hadn't even thought about that."

"Maybe we could conserve resources by having each child wear one glove – you know, on the hand they will use to pick things up? That way, everyone will be protected from germs."

Zedalla agreed, "Absolutely! I bet more students will help if they know they don't have to touch nasty trash with their bare hands."

"And I'll make sure that everyone washes their hands when they come back inside. Just as an extra precaution," suggested Miss Boyer.

"Great!" said Zedalla. "Thank you. I really appreciate it."

"You're welcome," said nurse Boyer. "See you tomorrow!"

Just then, Mrs. Singer opened her office door. She asked Zedalla to come in. They reviewed Zedalla's announcement outline together.

"This looks great. I think you're ready," said Mrs. Singer. "Just remember, your attitude is contagious. Be sure to show that unique Zedalla enthusiasm when you speak."

Zedalla nodded. She sat next to Mrs. Singer as she updated the school on the day's events. She fidgeted a little.

Then Mrs. Singer said, "I have a special guest here today with an important announcement. You may or may not know this student, but you have probably noticed her colorful personality around school. She has a great idea and I'd like you all to consider participating. Now, please give a listening ear to Zedalla Jones as she tells you about her project."

Zedalla spoke passionately, clearly, and enthusiastically about the clean-up.

"Hello, my name is Zedalla Jones. I am here today because I want to tell you about an important project that my friends and I created.

Here are a few of the important details:

What? It is called Project Plastic.

Why? We are doing Project Plastic for five main reasons. First, plastic garbage is a big problem because it ends up in the oceans. Second, animals can get hurt if they get caught in plastic fishing nets. Third, some animals die from eating plastic because they think it's food. Fourth, people use too much plastic just one time (like bottles or straws) and then throw it away. And, fifth, plastic never goes away. It stays on the earth for an extremely long time as ugly garbage.

How? We thought of an idea about how we can help solve the problem. We will clean up plastic garbage right here at school.

Where? The cleanup will be on our playground.

When? Friday during each lunch recess.

Who? Everyone is invited to participate in Project Plastic.

"One more thing… Just so you know, we will have gloves, so you don't have to touch the garbage. Please help us make our playground sparkle. Thank you."

Mrs. Singer patted Zedalla on the shoulder. "Well done," she said. "You are an eloquent speaker. I think you got your message across just perfectly."

"Thank you," said Zedalla. "I just hope other students will participate."

"Oh, they will," said Mrs. Singer. "You have a special way of motivating people through your example. And I'll stop by to see how things are going. That might help motivate them, too."

As Zedalla walked down the hallway toward homeroom, the first graders were on their way to the library. She didn't know many of them, but she always flashed a kind smile when she saw them.  This time, they pointed at her and waved.

"Hi, Zedalla!" they shouted. "Can we help pick up trash?"

Zedalla waved back and smiled. She made eye contact with their teacher, Mr. Overton. She had enjoyed being in his class, all those years ago. He must have told his students about Zedalla. She had quickly become a minor celebrity at school.

"Yes! You can all help," she responded. "I am so glad to hear that you will participate! Thank you!" She high-fived each first grader as she walked by.

As she entered her homeroom, she received a small round of applause and a few, "Woo-hoos!" Her teacher, Ms. Presley, praised Zedalla for a great job. She announced an increased recycling effort in her classroom. Zedalla thanked her.

At lunchtime, Zedalla refused the little plastic straw in the little plastic wrapper. Instead, she drank her milk right from the carton. She didn't even spill a drop. Tess, Olivia, and Nick refused straws, too. Zedalla and her friends watched as her other classmates followed their lead.

As Zedalla picked up her tray, she overheard one of the lunch ladies say, "Who needs straws anyway? They're used one time for ten minutes and then they go straight into the garbage. It's such a waste. I'm taking them off the next order."

My attitude IS contagious, she thought. Zedalla loved how the plastic project was taking off. Everyone was getting into it!

The friends sat at a table together and ate quickly. They had work to do.

As they dumped their trash, Mr. Norbert, the custodian, said, "I hear you need a garbage can for a playground pickup tomorrow. I'll have it waiting for you by the door."

"Thanks! And a recycling bin, too, please?" asked Tess.

They thanked Mr. Norbert with a fist-bump on the way out.

"Oh, yeah. Of course," replied Mr. Norbert. Then as he walked away, he mumbled to himself, "Come to think of it, we need a few more recycling bins around this school..."

This was great. People in all parts of the school were noticing what they could do. Each person had an idea about how to make a difference. Zedalla was excited by all the support.

Some of Zedalla's classmates had seen the news about the whale with plastic in its stomach, too. They were just as appalled as Zedalla, but they didn't know what to do about it. Or, maybe they didn't think they could make a difference. Zedalla knew they could. She was sure of it. She just had to convince them.

Chapter 19
The Big Day

Finally, Friday morning arrived. It was the day of the playground clean-up – Zedalla's plastic project. Her classmates and schoolmates didn't know it, but Zedalla knew today would be the start of something big. She couldn't wait to get started.

She woke up early. Earlier than normal. She simply couldn't sleep any more. She put on her T-shirt from the GPGP adventure and her comfiest pair of pants. She put on her special bracelet from Grandma G, and she even wore her Project Plastic bracelet. She grabbed two random socks and slipped on her favorite tennis shoes.

Zedalla went through the motions of breakfast, but probably had no idea what she was eating. Her mom wondered what was up with Zedalla. She seemed distracted, excited, and antsy about getting to school earlier than normal. Zedalla took a big, long, deep breath then shared the details of her plastic project with her mom.

135

She told her mom about the playground pick-up, the announcement, the flyers, and recycling bins in the classrooms.

Zedalla even explained how she stopped using plastic straws, and suddenly, her classmates stopped using straws, too. She described how everyone at school was following her ideas.

Initially, her mom was speechless. Then she asked Zedalla, "Did you start all of this? Was this your idea? You and your friends amaze me every day, Z. I am so impressed. You are becoming such an awesome, strong, and thoughtful young lady."

After a big hug from her mom, Zedalla was out the door.

"Have a fabulous day," her mom called after her.

"You too, Mom. I know it's going to be a fabulous day! For sure," said Zedalla. She had an extra spring in her step and an extra big smile on her face. It was a sunny day and it was perfect weather for a clean-up. She felt positive, happy, and excited. Nothing could stop her perfect mood.

Zedalla met up with Nick and Tess as she normally did. They were excited, too. And they were also wearing their bright blue shirts.

"You guys ready for the big clean-up?" asked Zedalla.

"Absolutely!" said Tess.

"For sure!" said Nick, "I'm ready to get down and dirty with some playground trash."

They met up with Olivia on the playground. She was ready with her bright blue shirt, too. They noticed lots of trash on the playground.

"We definitely need to do this," said Olivia. "In fact, we should probably clean up the entire school property, that is, if Mrs. Singer will let us."

"I'm pretty sure she wouldn't say no to that," said Nick. "I think she would be happy with whatever we do."

"Well, she said she'd be out there during the clean-up, so we can ask her then," said Zedalla.

"The reaction is awesome so far. We will have a lot of volunteers. I'm looking forward to it."

The morning bell rang. They slid down the slide and ran inside. As they separated to head to their homerooms, Zedalla called after them, "See you guys at recess!"

Today, the morning at school went super-fast. So fast that Zedalla didn't even look at the clock once to realize what time it was. Before she knew it, they were eating lunch. It felt like she had just eaten breakfast. Maybe she was a little nervous and excited about the clean-up, but she didn't feel like eating much.

When her friends were done eating, they got ready for the clean-up. They found Mr. Norbert at the back door with a garbage can and a recycling can, just where he said he would be. They rolled the cans outside.

Miss Boyer met them at the door with a box of eco-friendly gloves. She also brought some used plastic grocery bags.

"In case some kids want to partner up and collect trash then dump it in the big bin," she suggested. "It is so great that you're doing this," she said again and again. "It's such a wonderful idea! I am so proud of all of you."

They thanked her for the gloves and the bags. She remembered important things that they hadn't even thought of.

Zedalla's class and the first graders shared the first recess period. When the bell rang, the students made their way to the playground, and a line for gloves quickly formed. Nearly everyone wanted to participate.

Zedalla waited for the crowd of kids to quiet down.

Then she announced, "Thank you so much for helping us today. Please use your one glove to pick up trash, then bring it back, and put it in this bin. If you find any recyclables, like cans, paper, or glass bottles, place them in the recycle bin. Please do not pick up any broken glass or dangerous items! If you find anything sharp, let us know and we'll have an adult pick it up safely."

As she continued, students were off and running to find trash, "If some of you want to team up, you can have a small bag to share. When it starts to get full, you can bring it back, and dump it in the big bin, then go out and find some more."

Just as the clean-up was getting underway, Mrs. Singer appeared in the doorway to supervise. "You guys ordered the perfect weather for your clean-up today," she smiled. "And, it looks like almost all of the students are involved!"

"I'm just surprised how many students actually want to pick up trash," said Zedalla. "I'm also impressed. I mean, I didn't have to say or do much and everyone's just doing their part."

"That's the kind of leadership that works best – show your passion and lead by example," said Mrs. Singer. "I can already tell this project will be a great success."

Suddenly, Nick had more confidence than normal in speaking with school authority. Maybe it was because he felt so strongly about the clean-up. He wanted to make the most of the opportunity.

He cleared his throat and said, "Excuse me, Mrs. Singer, can we please extend the clean-up to all of the school grounds?"

Mrs. Singer glared at Nick. He froze. For a second, he thought he was in trouble. Again. His heart pounded. His face must have turned bright red. He waited.

Then she cracked a smile, and said, "That would be fabulous! What an awesome idea, Nick! Just make sure nobody is alone on one side of the school. A playground monitor should be there to supervise."

Nick breathed a sigh of relief. He wasn't in trouble at all. He had come up with a great idea. Phew.

"Done and done. I'll take a team this way," he said, pointing to the parking lot around the corner of the school.

Meanwhile, Tess and a small group took on another side of the school. Zedalla and Olivia monitored the playground clean-up, making sure that students knew what to do and how to sort their items into the correct bins – trash or recycling.

Every time someone put something in the bin or can, Zedalla said, "Thank you so much!"

Zedalla felt a little silly thanking people for trash, but as she thought about it some more, she realized she was really thanking them for their help and support. And for keeping the playground and the environment clean. And for keeping some trash out of the oceans. So, she kept saying, "Thank you."

The clean-up went quickly. Zedalla noticed that kids were actually having fun while they were picking up trash together! It almost didn't seem like work. They were like actually coming together as a team. As a school.

Soon the bell rang, and the first recess was over. They had already collected almost an entire can full of trash. And lots of recyclables, too.

The students lined up to go inside. As promised, Miss Boyer led them to the bathroom to wash their hands before sending them off to class.

Nick announced, "I think that's it. We got everything. Doesn't it look clean?"

Zedalla was excited by all the hard work. "Seriously?! Wow! It does look amazing. Are you sure there is nothing left to pick up?"

Nick ran a quick lap around the school to double-check and returned out of breath. "Yep, clean as a whistle," he reported between gasps.

Now Zedalla was a little worried that there wasn't any trash left for the next recess group to pick up, at least there wasn't any more trash today. Zedalla knew that if there wasn't any trash left, then the job was done and they didn't need more volunteers.

Zedalla believed that everyone should have the chance to volunteer and help if they wanted to. That was important to her. She didn't want anyone to feel left out. If there wasn't any trash left, what could they do instead? She thought quickly and decided to write a short list of other ways students could help.

Zedalla borrowed a pen and paper from Olivia and wrote the first few ideas that came to mind:

Easy ways to help reduce plastic use:
1. Stop using plastic straws.
2. Reuse plastic bags, bottles, and other plastic things (like containers).
3. Use fabric grocery bags. Or reuse bags.
4. Bring clean plastic containers to the art room.
5. Pick up trash in your neighborhood.
6. Recycle what you can.
7. Put trash where it belongs!

When the next group of students came out for recess, they were enthusiastic and ready to work.

"Hi, Zedalla!" they shouted, "We want to help clean up plastic and trash."

Zedalla hesitated. She was nervous. They were so excited. She didn't want to let them down.

"Just tell them," said Mrs. Singer, gently placing her hand on Zedalla's shoulder.

Zedalla explained that the first recess had so many volunteers that there was no trash left to pick up. She thanked them for their enthusiasm and support. She promised them that another day, they would have a chance to help clean up the playground.

She read her list of easy ways to reduce plastic use.

"These are simple things you CAN do today to help the environment," she added. "They are just as important as cleaning up the playground."

Zedalla continued, " You can make a big difference if you do just one of these things from my list."

As Zedalla spoke to the group of third and fourth graders, she watched their enthusiastic smiles turn into frowns of disappointment.

"What?" said one boy in disbelief.

"Seriously?" said a girl.

"Oh, man. That stinks. And to think, I was actually looking forward to picking up garbage," said another student.

But then something strange happened...

Chapter 20
No More Plastic!

From the back of the group of students, Zedalla heard a faint sound. It was almost like a song. Or a chant of some sort. She listened more closely. She held her finger up to her lips as if to shush the crowd. Everyone quieted and they listened, too.

One of the third-grade girls had started chanting, "No more plastic! No more plastic!"

She was moving and dancing to the beat of her own made-up tune. She bobbed her head back and forth and snapped her fingers, too. She was so lost in her own little world that she didn't realize everyone was looking at her. She just kept moving and her rhythm was rather catchy...

A few other students joined in the chant with her, "No more plastic! No more plastic!"

More and more students joined in. They started moving to the beat, too. The chant got louder and louder. Soon, everyone was chanting and dancing!

Tess had an idea. "Follow me," she told the third grader who had started the chant. They locked arms and Tess led her down the sidewalk.

Tess started marching with the girl, and the other students followed, still chanting. She had started a parade against plastic. More and more students followed. The parade got longer and longer. The chant got louder and louder.

"Awesome," Zedalla whispered to herself.

The teachers and students inside were distracted by the loud chanting and commotion. They stared out the windows at the plastic parade. They wanted to join in. So, they did.

Classes started trickling outside and jumped on the back of the parade. Eventually, there was a long line that extended all the way around the school. Everyone was chanting and marching.

"This is great!" exclaimed Nick and Olivia.

The response was unbelievable.

Mrs. Singer smiled and clapped her hands, "Wow. Just… wow. I love it!" Even she jumped into the parade line.

Zedalla beamed with pride. She had amazed herself. This was the start of her quest to make a difference in the world. She kissed each gem on her bracelet.

The red gem pulsed and glowed. Zedalla admired the beautiful light. "That's my gem!" she thought.

She realized that her passion was guiding her, and people were following because they felt it, too. All at once, Zedalla felt this overwhelming sense of responsibility. It was hard to explain, but she felt the power of her passion. She knew she had to share her passion with the world. She had this unique ability that not everyone had, and she had to use that power for positive change.

It didn't feel like a burden or a job though.
It felt... exciting. Inspiring. Invigorating. Motivating.
THIS was what passion felt like.

"Thank you, Grandma G," she said to the bracelet, as if it embodied Grandma's inspiration.

Little did Zedalla know that Grandma G was actually watching. She just happened to be driving by the school on her way to the grocery store. She heard the commotion in the school yard and pulled her car over to see what was going on.

"Well, check that out," she said, smiling to herself. "I bet my girl Zedalla's got something to do with this parade. I can feel it in my bones."

After watching for a few minutes, Grandma G pulled off and honked her horn in support. A few other cars did the same thing. Some students waved and hollered back, "Woo hoo!"

Zedalla knew that this was just the beginning of many adventures to come. She imagined what her friends might do next. Her mind started wandering into the future, but she quickly shook herself back to the current moment.

For right now, she wanted to watch and savor every bit of what was happening. She happily joined the very end of the parade so she could see the whole thing. She held her head up high and smiled with pride.

FOR MORE INFORMATION...

Dive in and learn more about oceans, plastic, animals, technology, conservation, plastic-free inventions, and what you can do to help.

To get your unique, recycled ocean plastic bracelet:
4 Ocean Plastic at https://www.4ocean.com

Promise: We pull one pound of trash from the ocean and coastlines for every product purchased.

~~~~~~~~~~~~~~~~~~~~~~~~~~~~~~~~~

To learn more about the GPGP (Great Pacific Garbage Patch):
visit https://theoceancleanup.com/great-pacific-garbage-patch

~~~~~~~~~~~~~~~~~~~~~~~~~~~~~~~~~

To learn about plastic in the oceans:
Ocean Conservancy at https://oceanconservancy.org
National Ocean Service at https://oceanservice.noaa.gov

~~~~~~~~~~~~~~~~~~~~~~~~~~~~~~~~~

To learn about ocean clean-up efforts, technology, and initiatives:
The Ocean Cleanup at https://theoceancleanup.com
Plastic Ocean Project at https://www.plasticoceanproject.org
National Geographic at https://www.nationalgeographic.com
Notpla at https://www.notpla.com

~~~~~~~~~~~~~~~~~~~~~~~~~~~~~~~~~

To learn more about oceans and animals:
Oceana at https://oceana.org
National Geographic for Kids at http://kids.nationalgeographic.com
Sea Legacy at https://www.sealegacy.org

Be an EVERYDAY HERO!
Do you want to get started rescuing oceans right now?

Start here

1. Pick up litter in your neighborhood.
2. Replace plastic shopping bags with reusable fabric bags.
3. Repurpose old plastic containers for crafts or storage.
4. Refuse straws or save your straw and use it again.
5. Rinse and reuse small plastic baggies.
6. Replace single-use plastic water bottles with a resuable and washable drinking bottle.
7. Recycle all plastic products that your city allows.
8. Choose products wrapped in paper, boxes, fabric, or compostable packaging.
9. Pay attention and keep track of how much plastic you use in one day, then cut down wherever you can.
10. Ask your friends and family to join you in rescuing oceans!

WHAT DO EVERYDAY HEROES THINK ABOUT?

Solving problems in the world always begins with someone asking a question and having a passion to create positive change.

That spark leads to more questions, discussion, exploration, experimentation, teamwork, and energy.
Which is to say... ACTION!

What action will you take to be an Everyday Hero?
Start with a question...

Think about these topics and questions...

1. Zedalla, Nick, Tess, and Olivia's adventure takes them to Hawaii.

• Find Hawaii on a map. What do you notice about Hawaii?

• What new information did you learn about Hawaii from the adventure in this story?

• What other information would like to know about Hawaii?

• If you have visited Hawaii, what was one of your favorite parts about that trip?

• How is Hawaii different from where you live?

2. Zedalla and her friends learn about the negative aspects of plastic, especially single-use plastics like straws, bags, and other items that are used only once before being thrown in the trash.

• Can you identify some plastic products or items that are only used once, or for a short period of time (less than 48 hours)?

• Can you identify examples of plastic products or items that are used for a long time (like 1, 5, 10 years, or more), or used several times before being thrown in the trash?

• Think about how long it takes plastic to break down once it is in the environment. Is there a difference in the length of time it takes for single-use or long-term plastics to break down once in the trash?

3. Zedalla, Nick, Olivia, and Tess solve problems throughout the story.

• How did problem-solving move them forward in their adventure?

• Did the friends differ in their approach to problems? If so, how?

• Do you think most people handle problems in the same way? Why or why not?

• How might people perceive problems differently? How does this affect how they approach or try to solve the problem?

• Do you think that people use different problem solving strategies? If so, are the differences positive or negative? Why?

4. After their adventure in Hawaii, the friends research and discover some great ways to reduce plastic waste from ending up in the ocean.

• Think about your daily life. How can you reduce your plastic use?

• How can you positively impact your house, school, or community?

• What can businesses and the government do to help reduce or eliminate plastic and plastic waste?

• How can people more effectively protect the oceans, animals, and the environment?

5. Grandma G gives Zedalla a bracelet that ends up being magical.

• Do you believe in magic? Why or why not?

• How was the magic activated in the story?

• The gemstones on Zedalla's bracelet represent passion, creativity, empathy, and wonderment. How do you show each quality?

• Where would you like magic to take you?

• What issue or problem would you like to learn more about?

• Which of your friends would make a great Everyday Hero? Why?

About the Creator of Zedalla™
and Everyday Heroes

Darci Fredricks

Darci is a successful business owner
and professional with a passion
to create positive changes in the world.

She loves traveling to interesting places,
caring for animals, and learning
about other cultures and how
others experience our world.

She lives in Portland, Oregon
with her husband and two dogs -
Stella and Dixie.

• •

About the Author/Illustrator
of Zedalla Jones and the Magical Stones

Joanna J. Robinson

Joanna is a freelance writer, illustrator,
and education professional.

She loves being creative, cooking, and
advocating for animals and children.

She lives in North Royalton, Ohio
with her husband and four cats -
Presley, Morris, Grover, and Moo.

https://jart1473.wixsite.com/joannarobinson

.

Made in USA - Kendallville, IN
1215992_9781736050101
12.29.2020 2256